REFLECTIOI
TOMORROW

One Woman's Journey to Rewrite Her Future

Copyright © 2024 by Mark Stone

All Rights Reserved.

ISBN: 9798339361985 (Paperback Edition)

Cover Image © Mark Stone

First Edition (30 September 2024)

No part of this book may be reproduced in any form or by any electronic or mechanical means, including information storage and retrieval systems, without written permission from the author, except for the user of a brief quotation in book reviews.

INTRODUCTION

What if the life you're living is only one possibility among countless others? What if the choices you've made are just reflections of paths you've never taken, lingering somewhere just beyond reach?

In **_Reflections of Tomorrow_**, the boundaries of reality blur, leaving one woman to question everything she thought she knew. As her world unravels, she must confront the unknown and face the unsettling truth: What if you could rewrite your story? What if your future wasn't set in stone?

PROLOGUE

"Embrace change as life's constant, for only by letting go can we become who we're meant to be."

Isabella rested against the railing of her balcony, the city's lights below weaving themselves into the shimmering fabric of life. The evening breeze caressed her skin, yet the tranquillity she sought remained elusive. Lately, reality had begun to blur at the edges of her perception, as if the world slipped out of focus when she wasn't watching. Unfamiliar memories haunted her—fleeting glimpses of another life, another version of herself. She hadn't confided in anyone about these visions; after all, who would believe her?

For years, she had lived according to others' expectations—diligent, accommodating, quietly suffocating in a relationship that had become more obligation than affection. Her husband was predictable to a fault. The youthful passion they once shared had faded into monotony. He took her presence for granted, and she had permitted it. What choice did she have?

What began as passing thoughts had intensified, intruding not only into her dreams but into her waking moments as well. Each vision grew more tangible, coming close enough to convince her they were real—yet she knew they weren't *her* memories. She felt threatened as they took their toll on her, shaking the foundations of her identity. The woman she had always known herself to be—logical, composed, anchored by routine—now felt like a stranger. She was becoming someone else. Someone bolder, freer. Someone she longed to embrace.

She had dismissed these experiences as mere fatigue from long hours at the lab. One night, while analysing data late into the evening, the lights flickered, and for an instant, she was elsewhere. The scent of pine and freshly fallen snow filled her senses, the crisp cold biting at her cheeks. The memory was vivid but did not belong to her. Then she blinked, and she was back in the lab, clutching at fragments she couldn't comprehend.

Day by day, the woman she thought she knew was being rewritten, drawing her toward lives she hadn't lived. The face in the mirror appeared different now, her eyes inviting in the woman she didn't recognise but was eager to know.

Standing on the balcony, she felt it again—a subtle tremor, as if something were just out of reach. Her reflection shimmered, blurring momentarily. Fragments of another existence surfaced. She saw herself in a different place, bathed in moonlight, a stranger beside her—his presence both comfortingly familiar and thrillingly new. The sensation was so real it stole her breath away.

"What is happening to me?" she whispered, her fingers tightening around the railing.

01 – A NEW DAWN

" Life's journey often brings us back to where we began, seeing it anew with wiser eyes."

The Daystrom Institute's Annual Gala Night, Sky Gardens, 20 Fenchurch Street, London, EC3M 8AF - 8:30 PM, February 11

The annual Daystrom Institute Gala was an affair where champagne flowed endlessly and guests arrived in chauffeured cars, stepping onto the red carpet like film stars. The sleek entrance to the Sky Garden, perched 155 meters above London, was flanked by photographers and reporters vying for glimpses of the night's most prestigious attendees. Clad in designer gowns and bespoke suits, the city's elite spilled into the night —politicians, tech magnates, and scientists converging under one dazzling roof.

Adjusting her dress, Isabella stepped onto the carpet with James beside her, his grin widening as cameras flashed. To the world, they appeared the perfect couple, but to her, this was merely another event in a long line of performances. Tonight wasn't about them; it was about Daystrom and celebrating its success.

Inside, anticipation buzzed in the air. Guests mingled beneath the vast glass canopy of the Sky Garden, surrounded by lush greenery and panoramic views of the London skyline. Waiters glided through the crowd, offering champagne flutes and delicate canapés. The hum of conversation filled the space, punctuated by bursts of laughter and the clinking of glasses.

Upon arrival, they were guided through security, but a flicker on the system caught the attendant's eye. Isabella was already registered as present? The attendant frowned briefly, but Ted Barker, Director of Research at the Daystrom Institute, had already spotted them.

"Ah, there you are!" came a familiar voice. Ted Barker, every inch the polished executive in his tailored tuxedo, approached with a smile. "You both look splendid. Come, let's get a drink, shall we? We have quite the evening ahead." He dismissed the security glitch with an offhand gesture and took Isabella by the arm.

"Quite the crowd tonight," James remarked, scouring the room. Isabella held back a sigh. They had only just arrived, and already he seemed distracted. The growing distance between them was palpable, his attention always drifting elsewhere at these events.

"It's not every day we have half the Cabinet rubbing shoulders with Silicon Valley's finest," Ted replied with a grin. "Even Lord Davenport is here somewhere—still championing that AI policy of his."

Isabella noticed how effortlessly Ted navigated the sea of influential faces. Just over his shoulder, Davina Drake, head of Obsidian Industries, was charming her way through a circle of government officials. Davina's presence was impossible to ignore—ruthless and glamorous, she had a reputation for being both brilliant and formidable. She had been Daystrom's fiercest competitor for years, and tonight she seemed intent on reminding everyone of that fact.

"The infamous Davina Drake," James muttered, admiration in his tone. "I wonder who she's planning to impress tonight?"

"Everyone," Isabella replied tersely.

As they ventured deeper into the venue, the excitement grew. It wasn't just the glamour or the high-profile guests—it was the whispers about what was to be unveiled. The Daystrom Institute had long been at the forefront of scientific discovery, but tonight felt different. Tonight, they would offer the world a glimpse of the future.

The lights dimmed slightly, and a soft chime signalled guests to gather near the stage. Ted, ever the consummate host, stepped up to the podium, commanding attention with ease.

"Ladies and gentlemen, welcome to the Daystrom Institute's Annual Gala," he began, the sound resonating throughout the hall. "Tonight, we're not just celebrating another year of achievements; we're celebrating the future—our future—and the incredible minds shaping it."

Applause rippled through the audience, the excitement tangible.

"Many of you know that Daystrom has led the way in medical and scientific innovation for over a decade," Ted continued. "What you may not know is that we're on the verge of something revolutionary, something that will redefine not just our industry but humanity's understanding of its place in the universe."

A hush settled over the crowd, all eyes fixed on him. This was the moment they had anticipated—the hint of something groundbreaking.

"And so, it is my absolute pleasure to introduce the visionary behind this extraordinary leap forward," Ted declared grandly. "Mr. Zach Mondori, lead scientist of our Quantum Bridge Project."

Zach stepped onto the stage to enthusiastic applause, his demeanour calm and assured. Not one to seek the limelight, he accepted it gracefully tonight. Tall and composed, he approached the podium and began to speak.

"Thank you, Ted, and thank you all for joining us this evening," he said, his words measured. "I won't reveal all our secrets—at least not yet. But I can tell you that we stand on the edge of a new frontier. The Quantum Bridge Project is unlike anything we've encountered before. It's a technology that will allow us to peer beyond our current understanding of space and time. Believe me when I say, the possibilities are endless."

The room remained silent, captivated by the promise of what lay ahead. Zach didn't delve into technicalities—it wasn't the night for that. Instead, he left them hanging on his every word, tantalised by the prospect of a future reshaped by his work.

As he left the stage, the crowd erupted in applause, awe and anticipation mingling in the air. Isabella joined in, watching as Zach disappeared into the throng, fielding handshakes and questions from all sides.

Meanwhile, James had drifted away, as he often did, toward the clusters of admirers that flocked to such events. His charm was effortless, but beneath it lay insecurities that only Isabella truly understood. His flirtations were a game, a façade masking his own doubts. She observed him from a distance, the familiar hollow feeling inside. Tonight, it stung more than usual. When it was time to leave, there would be the inevitable argument—a pattern they seemed unable to break.

Davina continued to work the room, making it clear that Obsidian Industries had no intention of lagging behind Daystrom in the race to dominate the biotech sector. Her conversations were strategic and fluid as she moved between tech moguls and politicians, ensuring her presence was felt at every turn.

Seeking respite, Isabella joined a group of Daystrom scientists engaged in animated discussion. It was there she first encountered Maggie Carter. A name somehow familiar to her. Poised and magnetic, the woman exuded a sharp intelligence that drew others in. Ted noticed her too, his interest piqued. The woman's grasp of quantum mechanics was nearly unparalleled—a rare find. He made a note to learn more about her affiliations.

As the conversation shifted to more mundane topics, Isabella excused herself and stepped onto a quiet balcony, inhaling the crisp night air. The soft glow from the ballroom spilled out, casting a gentle light around her. Below, London sprawled in all its nocturnal splendour, but it was the star-studded sky that drew her gaze. Up here, high above the streets, she felt a fleeting sense of freedom, her thoughts drifting with the evening breeze.

Moments later, someone approached—the man who had captivated the audience earlier. He neared her, clearing his throat softly as he offered her a glass of champagne.

"You shouldn't be out here without a drink in hand," Zach remarked warmly, his eyes twinkling with the subtlest hint of mischief.

Startled, she turned to him, and their eyes met. He was impeccably dressed, his dark hair and olive complexion highlighting eyes that caught the light in an intriguing way. There was an effortless charm about him, a quiet intensity that almost thrilled.

"Thank you," she replied, accepting the glass. She was pleasantly surprised at his easy manner. "I should have known better at an event like this."

He tilted his head thoughtfully. "Isabella Keane, isn't it? Leading the *New Dawn* project—Alzheimer's research?"

She nodded, intrigued that he knew her name. "That's right. And you're Zach Mondori—the man everyone's talking about tonight."

A soft chuckle escaped him as he leaned against the railing beside her. "It seems I can't escape my reputation. I've heard about your work as well—impressive stuff. There's some interesting overlap between your research and mine."

Her eyebrows lifted in curiosity. "Quantum entanglement and Alzheimer's? Perhaps. Some of my recent studies are loosely based on the paper you and Ted published a couple of years ago."

"You'd be surprised," he continued. "The human mind, memory, time itself—they're more interconnected than most people realise. My team has observed some... unexpected correlations when we push the boundaries."

She sipped her champagne, the effervescence tickling her senses as she pondered his words. The way he spoke —with quiet confidence and certainty—drew her in. After so long merely going through the motions of life, she felt truly engaged, no longer just playing the role others expected of her.

"Unexpected correlations?" she echoed, a spark of interest lighting her eyes. "It sounds like you're onto something remarkable."

He smiled, his gaze holding hers. "We might be."

Their conversation hovered in that space, teetering between professional intrigue and something more personal. Isabella felt the pull of it—the ease with which they connected, the shared excitement over ideas. It felt strangely comfortable, as if they had known each other far longer than these brief moments.

And then, fate interrupted their moment.

The sound of raised voices cut through the ambient

murmurs from inside. Isabella glanced over her shoulder, her heart sinking as she recognised one of the voices—James.

Zach followed her gaze, a slight crease forming on his brow as the commotion grew louder. She turned fully to see James, his face flushed, and posture unsteady, engaged in a heated exchange with another guest who appeared equally agitated.

A weary sigh escaped her. The pleasant, effortless interaction with Zach dissipated as reality intruded once more.

"I'm sorry," she murmured, offering an apologetic smile while handing back the half-finished glass. "I need to..."

He accepted the glass with a gentle nod. "No explanation necessary."

She cast him a final, lingering glance before weaving her way through the crowd, each step laden with resignation.

Zach remained on the balcony, watching until she disappeared from view. His gaze lingered on the doorway, not wishing to let the feeling fade.

Turning back to the panoramic cityscape, he sipped his champagne. The beauty of the night enveloped him, but his thoughts remained with her, drifting like the quiet night breeze.

***

The Keane residence, Russell Square Mansions, 12 Russell Square, Bloomsbury, London, WC1B 5BG - 11:50 PM, February 11

Isabella unlocked the door and stepped into the apartment, her heels resonating softly on the parquet floor as she flicked on the light. A tired, end-of-day sigh escaped her lips; the evening pressed heavily upon her shoulders. She slipped off her shoes, feeling the coolness of the wood beneath her feet. Behind her, James stumbled in, his tie askew, muttering under his breath. The smell of alcohol clung to him, the night's indulgence lingering like a bitter haze.

"Great night, wasn't it?" he slurred, sarcasm dripping from each word. "All those people fawning over you, acting like I didn't even exist."

She remained silent, her back to him as she hung up her coat. The familiar pattern was unfolding once more. Throughout the evening, she had sensed it building—the sidelong glances, the forced smiles, his flirtations with women who found his charm amusing until they didn't.

"Are you going to say something?" he demanded. "Or will you just stand there pretending everything's perfect?"

Turning to face him, she held his gaze with tired eyes. "What can I say, James? That you made a spectacle of yourself? That you embarrassed me?" Her tone was calm, but a thread of frustration wove through it.

He glared, stepping closer. "Oh, so it's my fault now, is it? Always blaming me. You can't stand me talking to another woman without getting all…"

"I'm not jealous," she interrupted, her voice sharpening. "I'm tired. Tired of watching you make a fool of yourself night after night. Flirting, drinking, acting like none of it matters. Then you expect me to pretend everything is fine."

"Maybe I'm sick of this!" he retorted, gesturing wildly. "This sham of a marriage! You're always working, always at that blasted lab. You don't care about us anymore!"

Her eyes narrowed as the anger inside her igniting. "Don't you dare blame my work for this. I've been holding us together for years while you've been chasing distractions. I'm done pretending."

He scoffed, bitterness twisting his expression. "Oh, you're done, are you? Think you can just walk away from everything we've built?"

She folded her arms, her voice turning cold. "I'm not the one who walked away. You did, a long time ago."

His face tensed further, and he took another step forward, but she stood her ground.

"You're drunk," she said quietly. "I won't do this tonight. You have a flight to Brussels in the morning. Sleep in the guest room."

His eyes widened in disbelief. "You're throwing me out of our bedroom now?"

Without another word, she turned away, heading toward the kitchen. "You've been absent in every way that matters for years. The least you can do is give me some peace tonight. I don't want to see you like this."

His hands clenched at his sides, knuckles whitening. The tension hung thick in the air.

"I'm fed up with this—fed up with you," he spat, his words laced with venom. "This whole life... it's suffocating me."

She paused, her back still to him, a pang of sadness piercing her heart. But she wouldn't let him see it.

"Then go," she whispered. "Go to Brussels. Go wherever you want. Just leave me be." With a trembling hand, she slipped off her wedding ring and set it down. This time, it might well be over.

He stared, a mixture of anger and shock crossing his

features. There was nothing left to say. With a bitter curse under his breath, he stormed away, the door to the guest room slamming shut behind him.

Alone in the quiet of the kitchen, she leaned on the counter, the cool surface reassuring. The echoes of their anger still lingered, but amidst the turmoil, she felt something stir—a faint spark flickering to life.

A whisper of infinite possibilities.

02 - HIDDEN FROM SIGHT

" What we perceive as reality is but a veil over deeper truths yet unseen."

The Keane residence, Russell Square Mansions, 12 Russell Square, Bloomsbury, London, WC1B 5BG - 07:00 AM, February 12

Isabella awoke abruptly, her skin damp with a thin sheen of perspiration, her mind grasping at the fading tendrils of a dream that felt more real than reality itself. That familiar sensation lingered—the feeling of being somewhere different, and her being someone else. This time, she had been in a dimly lit room adorned with rich Victorian décor. He was there beside her, a presence both comforting and exhilarating. Her arms had wrapped around his waist, her skin tingling from the playful touch of his fingers grazing her neck with a sharp, electrifying caress.

But already, the edges of the memory were dissolving, slipping away as the dawn pulled her back to the confines of her own life.

As the haze lifted, her bedroom came into focus—the well-worn poster of Albert Einstein, the clothes neatly folded into two piles, his and hers, waiting for someone to put them away. Daylight seeped past the blackout blinds, casting its soft glow on the occupant. Outside, birdsong filled the air—a reminder of one of the few perks of city living: the delicate balance between towering office blocks and the green spaces scattered throughout London.

She yawned, stretching her limbs in an attempt to shake off the stubborn weariness that clung to her. Fleeting thoughts of the argument with James the night before tried to surface, but she pushed them aside. It wasn't the first time, and likely wouldn't be the last. Instead, the dream she'd had took precedence. Normally, such nocturnal visions faded quickly upon waking, but this one had left an imprint. Perhaps it was the result of weeks of stress at work, or maybe one too many glasses of champagne at the gala.

Lying there beneath the tangled sheets, she gazed into the mirror, half-expecting to see a stranger staring back. But no, it was just her—the same features, the same figure, the same sense of being boxed in. A woman who had always played by society's rules, choosing safety over desire; the flames of passion smothered beneath layers of responsibility and routine, especially where James was concerned. Yet she had never known any other way.

"Midlife crisis," she muttered to herself, more statement than question. With a pang of heartache, she turned away from the mirror. It was time to rise and face the day—duty called.

Her thoughts returned to her daily routine and to Katie, still asleep in the room down the hall. At seventeen, her daughter had begun to pull away, as teenagers often do. But lately, the distance felt deeper, more personal, as if Isabella were losing touch with the one person she thought she could always rely on. Katie had been the mature one during the initial marital troubles, offering comfort in her own quiet way. But now, as things had settled into a strained normalcy at home, the gap between them had widened again, and Isabella had no idea why.

A sharp knock on the door interrupted her thoughts. A bleary-eyed teenager leaned against the frame, her hair tousled, sleep still clinging to her features.

"Mum, you were talking in your sleep again," Katie mumbled, rubbing her eyes.

Isabella felt a flush of embarrassment. "I'm sorry, sweetheart. Did I wake you?" Even as she asked, she knew it was a futile question. Katie shrugged in that quintessentially adolescent way.

"Kind of hard not to notice," she replied. "You sounded... different, like you were having an intense conversation or *something*. It was weird."

Her emphasis on the word *'something'* made Isabella's cheeks warm even more. What had she been saying?

"Just a bad dream," she said, attempting a reassuring smile. "Nothing to worry about. You should try to get some more sleep—you look tired. Were you up late studying again?" She hoped to steer the conversation away.

Katie hesitated, as if contemplating whether to press further, then nodded. "Yeah, something like that. Maybe you should get more rest too. You seem… distracted lately." Her tone masked concern behind a casual facade.

Before she could reply, Katie added with a faint smirk, "And maybe consider wearing a robe in the mornings. Just a thought."

With that final remark and a playful glint in her eye, she turned and headed back down the hall, leaving Isabella standing there, momentarily speechless.

Glancing at the clock, a surge of panic hit her. Late again! Why hadn't the alarm gone off? No time for breakfast—she had to get ready for work, and quickly.

***

The Daystrom Institute, Level 75, Meridian Tower, 12 Meridian Place, Canary Wharf, London - *09:22 AM, February 12*

Arriving precisely twenty-two minutes behind schedule, Isabella stepped out of the lift onto the gleaming, albeit sterile, floor of the Quantum Science Division. The tang of antiseptic mingled with the faint hum of machinery, a symphony of precision and control. Colleagues moved with purpose, their white lab coats crisp and unwrinkled, their expressions a blend of focus and fatigue.

Several stories above, executives likely gathered in their glass-walled offices, discussing strategies and the latest bids from competitors. They were the corporate grey-suits—rarely smiling, always orchestrating from behind the scenes like conductors of an invisible symphony.

Adjusting the strap of her bag, Isabella headed toward her workstation, her footsteps echoing softly on the polished floor. Once, this environment had brought her comfort—the orderliness, the predictability. Now, it felt oppressive, mirroring the stagnation she felt in other parts of her life.

Waiting by her desk was Ted Barker, arms crossed, his expression unreadable. Beside him stood a woman she had seen only a handful of times—Davina Drake from Obsidian Industries, an occasional partner but more often a direct competitor. Davina's presence was both unexpected and unsettling.

"Isabella," Ted said curtly. "Late again? We need a

progress update."

She set her bag down, steeling herself for the conversation. "I apologise," she replied evenly. "I've been reviewing the latest data. I can have a detailed report for you later today."

Ted's eyes narrowed. "By midday. The board is getting restless. We're behind schedule, and you know what that means."

She nodded, feeling the pressure mounting. The *New Dawn* project—her passion, her life's work—was under scrutiny. Developing a potential cure for Alzheimer's was no small feat, but the pressure to deliver results was mounting.

"There have been some… minor anomalies in the behavioural responses of the volunteers," she admitted. "I'm looking into it."

"Anomalies?" His tone sharpened. "What kind of anomalies?"

She hesitated, choosing her words carefully. "Subtle irregularities. Nothing definitive yet, but enough to warrant further investigation."

Ted exchanged a quick glance with Davina, whose expression remained impassive. "We can't afford delays," he said firmly. "Identify the issue and resolve it. Quickly."

"Understood," Isabella replied, suppressing the frustration that simmered barely beneath the surface.

Without another word, Ted turned and walked away, Davina following with a brief, enigmatic look in Isabella's direction.

Exhaling slowly, she sank into her chair. The screen before her blurred slightly as she blinked back the weariness threatening to overtake her. The project's importance was undeniable, but lately, the drive that had fuelled her was waning. She felt adrift, the purpose that once anchored her now uncertain.

"Rough morning?"

She looked up to see Emma, a colleague and occasional confidante, leaning casually against the partition. Emma's bright smile and easy demeanour were a welcome contrast to the tension that permeated the lab.

"You could say that" Isabella replied, mustering the slightest hint of a smile.

"Ted on the warpath again?" Emma asked, stepping into the workspace with two cups of coffee in hand.

"Nothing new there," Isabella said, accepting the offering gratefully. "Thanks."

"Don't let him get to you," Emma said, perching on the

desk. "You're brilliant at what you do. He knows it, even if he won't admit it."

Isabella took a sip, the warmth spreading through her hands. "Sometimes I wonder if it's worth it," she confessed quietly.

Emma studied her. "You ever think about shaking things up a bit? Taking a risk or two?"

"What, at work?" queried Isabella.

"At work, at home—anywhere," Emma said with a shrug. "Sometimes we get so comfortable in our routines that we forget there's a whole world out there."

Isabella suddenly felt like joining in the rebellion of her younger colleague. "Maybe I will."

A mischievous glint appeared in Emma's eyes. "By the way, interesting choice of accessories today."

"Accessories?"

Emma gestured subtly toward Isabella's neck. "Unless I'm mistaken, those look like scratch marks. Had an eventful night?"

Isabella's hand flew to her neck, fingertips brushing over the faint lines she hadn't noticed before. Heat rose to her cheeks. "I... must have scratched myself in my sleep."

"Must have been some dream," Emma teased, winking playfully. "Well, if you ever want to talk about it—or anything else—you know where to find me."

With that, she slipped away, leaving Isabella perplexed.

Turning back to her computer, Isabella's thoughts drifted. The scratches, the vivid dreams, the unsettling feeling that reality was shifting ever so slightly—it all meshed into a curious puzzle she needed to solve.

She pulled up the latest data sets, determined to focus, but the numbers seemed to dance across the screen, refusing to settle into coherent patterns.

Perhaps Emma was right. Perhaps it was time to consider the possibilities she had long dismissed.

How on earth had she ended up with scratches on her neck?

03 – LA DOLCE VITA

"Our choices shape our destiny, moulding us into who we become."

The Dolce Vita Café, 2A Kensington High Street, London W8 4PT - 12:00 PM, February 14

Zach Mondori sat outside his favourite café at one corner of Kensington Gardens, the late afternoon sun casting long, golden shadows across the verdant expanse before him. The gentle hum of passersby, the distant laughter of children, and the clinking of coffee cups should have brought him a measure of peace. Yet his mind was elsewhere.

He gazed at the untouched espresso before him, lost in memories that felt worlds apart from the serene scene surrounding him. *La Dolce Vita*, the café was called—a name promising the sweet life, though it had been a long time since he'd tasted such sweetness. Life, he mused, could be a fickle companion.

His thoughts drifted, as they often did, back to his research—success edging ever closer. The mysteries of science had always captivated him, especially the notion that particles could be intertwined regardless of distance or time, defying conventional understanding.

What had begun as a theoretical pursuit had transformed into something far more profound—a new beginning for science. Not a bad achievement for the son of immigrants.

But one hurdle remained. The random variations that grew more pronounced at higher intensities troubled him. He had tried to dismiss them as data errors or miscalculations, but the mounting evidence suggested otherwise. An inexplicable variable hiding in plain sight, and with it a growing unease.

Exhaling sharply, he slicked back his hair. Recent months had blurred into a whirlwind of long days and sleepless nights, poring over endless streams of data. No discernible pattern emerged from the anomalies. It felt as if the universe were playing a game of hide and seek, and he was perpetually one step behind.

Leaning back, he surveyed the park. Families picnicking, couples strolling hand in hand—it all seemed so normal, so distant from the inner turmoil consuming him. He longed for that simplicity, the comfort of being in the right place, at the right time, with the right person. Since the accident, inner peace had eluded him, and now he spent his days wrestling with the secrets of the cosmos.

A soft vibration pulled his attention to his phone. A message from a colleague at the facility—more data points that didn't align with their predictions. He should have been alarmed, but a deep-seated weariness made it difficult to summon concern.

Closing his eyes, he let the sounds of the gardens wash over him. For a brief moment, he allowed himself to drift, to forget everything. He yearned to feel normal again, to reconnect with the man he once was—before breakthroughs and obsessions had consumed his life.

The quick tempo of approaching footsteps drew him back. Opening his eyes, he saw her—the woman he'd met on the balcony the previous night.

She moved with effortless grace across the street, her hair catching the sunlight and shimmering like the purest silver. There was something about her that captivated him, holding his gaze firmly. Despite their brief encounter, it felt as though he knew her intimately.

His heartbeat quickened as she drew nearer. Oblivious to his presence, her focus was elsewhere, yet the closer she came, the stronger the inexplicable pull he felt toward her.

As she passed by, he considered calling out, inviting her to join him. But the words caught in his throat, and she continued on, unaware of the effect she had stirred within him.

He sighed, unable to shake the sensation that their paths had crossed before—somewhere, somehow. It was illogical, of course; he would have remembered meeting someone like her.

Watching her disappear into the throng, the feeling lingered like an echo. In that fleeting moment, he was certain she had sensed it too—that same connection. But the opportunity had slipped away, leaving him with a pang of regret.

Glancing at his watch, he realised his lunch break was over. Leaving a tip beside the untouched cup, he headed toward the overground station. As he rose, an unexpected gust of wind sent a chill through the air. Pulling his jacket closer, he resumed his journey, thoughts inevitably returning to his work. The more he pondered, the more convinced he became that an unseen force was influencing the results. In science, everything was connected.

***

Zach's Apartment, Meridian Court, 32 Greenwich High Road, London SE10 8JL – 09:50 PM, February 14

Later that evening, Zach sat at his desk in his flat, surrounded by scattered papers and half-empty cups of coffee. The glow from his computer screen bathed the room in a cold, sterile light, casting elongated shadows on the walls. He had been working for hours—running calculations, revisiting old data—but his mind kept returning to that moment in Kensington Gardens.

The way she had moved, the fleeting eye contact, the inexplicable feeling that their lives were already entwined.

He shook his head, attempting to dispel the distraction, and refocused on the task at hand. The larger they scaled the system, the greater the variances became. He had mapped them meticulously, traced points of convergence, yet a solution remained elusive. There was a missing piece—a variable he couldn't identify.

A sudden ring of the doorbell startled him. Glancing at the clock, he noted the lateness of the hour. He wasn't expecting visitors, especially not at this time, and the building's security was typically stringent. Pushing back his chair, he approached the door with a mix of curiosity and caution.

Part opening it, he found himself face-to-face with an unfamiliar man. Tall and rough-edged, the stranger exuded an air that immediately put Zach on alert. Dressed in a sharp suit and carrying a sleek briefcase, he looked both official and out of place.

"Mr. Mondori," the man said smoothly, his words honed into a well-practiced recital. "I represent Obsidian Industries. I believe you're aware of our partnership with the Daystrom Institute."

Of course, he'd heard of Obsidian—an organisation involved in some of the more classified facets of his research. He had always maintained a deliberate distance; something about them felt off—too secretive, too powerful.

" Obsidian? Yes, I'm aware of them." Zach replied cautiously. "What brings you here?"

"I'd like to discuss the variances you've been encountering," the man continued, his gaze steady.

Zach's grip tightened on the door. "And how exactly do you know about those?" His tone was measured, masking the unease he felt.

"We have our sources," the stranger said with a dismissive shrug. He stepped forward slightly, an unspoken expectation of being invited inside. "May I come in? Or would you prefer to discuss sensitive matters on your doorstep?"

Every instinct urged Zach to refuse, to close the door and end the conversation. This man, with his impeccable attire and practiced smile, radiated corporate manipulation. Yet as their eyes locked, Zach understood that this was not a request one could easily decline. Obsidian Industries wasn't known for accepting 'no' gracefully.

Reluctantly, he stepped aside. "Very well."

The man entered with a confident stride, his movements

calculated, as if he already owned the space. His eyes swept over the cluttered room—the scattered papers, the whiteboards filled with complex equations, the remnants of his relentless pursuit. An atmosphere of unspoken tension settled between them.

"Your research is remarkable," the man began, turning to face Zach. "A genuine breakthrough. But you know that." He paused, studying Zach's reaction before continuing. "We're particularly interested in the latest data you've gathered. We believe it holds the key to something much larger."

Zach remained standing, arms crossed defensively. "I'm not at liberty to discuss the specifics of my work, especially with those outside Daystrom."

An eyebrow arched slightly as the man settled into a chair without invitation. "We're not just any external party, Zach. Obsidian possesses resources far exceeding what Daystrom can offer. We could help you delve deeper, push boundaries you haven't even imagined. Unlock the full potential of your Quantum Bridge. But to do so, we need access to your findings."

Zach's unease deepened. "My research is off-limits. That's non-negotiable."

The man's composed façade flickered, replaced by a steely gaze. "We're not proposing a simple collaboration. This is an opportunity for mutual advancement. Think of what you could achieve with our support."

Zach took a deliberate step back. "I've seen what happens when Obsidian gets involved. Projects become distorted, repurposed beyond recognition. I won't allow that to happen to my work."

A long silence stretched between them. The man's patience seemed to wane as he rose slowly from the chair, adjusting his suit jacket with meticulous care. "I understand your reservations, but let me clarify." He moved closer, "This data—it's imperative that we obtain it. Preferably with your cooperation."

"Is that a threat?" Zach could hear his heart pounding.

"Consider it a candid assessment of the situation." The man's smile was thin, devoid of warmth. "We prefer collaboration. It's more efficient. But if you choose to be uncooperative, we'll have to explore alternative methods."

"Get out." Zach's voice was firm, the words leaving no room for misinterpretation.

The stranger held his gaze for longer than necessary, then inclined his head slightly. "Very well. But remember, Zach, our offer stands. It's in everyone's best interest to work together."

He moved toward the door, pausing with his hand on the

handle. "We'll be in touch. I'd advise reconsidering your position before things become, let's just say *complicated*."

The door closed with a decisive click, but the oppressiveness of the encounter lingered. Zach stood rooted to the spot, a myriad of thoughts racing through his mind. He knew with unsettling certainty that this was far from over.

Returning to his desk, he gazed blankly at the array of numbers and symbols before him. The sanctuary of his work now felt compromised. Obsidian's interest wasn't just a professional inconvenience—it was a looming threat.

He felt tense, the beginnings of a headache forming. The variances in his research, the inexplicable anomalies—they suddenly seemed entwined with forces beyond mere scientific curiosity. And now, with Obsidian's shadow cast over him, the stakes had risen dramatically.

Leaning back, he stared at the ceiling, exhaling slowly. He needed a plan, a way to safeguard his work and perhaps even himself. Isolation was no longer an option. Trusting his instincts, he realised there might be someone who could help—someone who shared his passion for discovery and perhaps understood the complexities he faced.

His thoughts drifted once more to the woman from the gala and outside the café. There was a connection there, an unspoken understanding he couldn't quite explain. Maybe reaching out to her wasn't just a personal desire but a necessary step in navigating the challenges ahead.

As the night deepened, Zach resolved to take action. Whatever was unfolding, he wouldn't face it passively. The complexities of his research had just intertwined with the complexities of his life.

He intended to face them head-on.

04 – BRIDGING THE DIVIDE

" Science melds reason with the passion and romance that fuels discovery.""

The Daystrom Institute, Level 22, Meridian Tower 12 Meridian Place Canary Wharf, London E14 9PL - 09:45 AM, February 16

The flickering lights in Zach Mondori's lab cast a soft glow over the array of cutting-edge equipment. He stood before his creation—a compact desktop prototype of the Quantum Bridge that represented years of tireless work. His eyes were fixed on the control panel as he made precise adjustments, aware that a single miscalculation could unravel everything. Today was critical; he could feel it.

Behind him, the lab door slid open with a quiet hiss. Without turning, Zach recognised the familiar presence of Ted Barker, Daystrom's Director of Research and his most trusted mentor.

"How's our revolutionary endeavour progressing?" Ted inquired, folding his arms as he approached.

Zach glanced up, his train of thought interrupted. "We're making strides. The prototype is holding steady. We transmitted a biological sample yesterday."

Ted's eyebrows lifted in surprise. "A biological sample? That's a significant leap forward."

"It is," Zach agreed, his expression turning more serious. "But we're still facing challenges. The sample experiences accelerated aging—about five years either way through the bridge."

Ted leaned in, scrutinizing the data on the screen. "So, temporal distortion is still affecting organic matter?"

"Exactly," Zach confirmed. "It's as if crossing the bridge compresses time for the object. We're working on counteracting that effect."

Ted nodded thoughtfully. "But the fact that you can send living tissue through at all is monumental. What possibilities does this open up?"

Zach's eyes brightened at the question. "Imagine instantaneous transportation of medical supplies to disaster zones, or organ transplants delivered across the globe in seconds. Beyond that, the Quantum Bridge could potentially allow us to explore places we can't physically reach—other dimensions or parallel realities."

Ted whistled softly. "You're talking about redefining the very boundaries of human experience."

"That's the goal," Zach said, his enthusiasm palpable. "But we need to stabilise the bridge to make it practical. Right now, the more power we use to sustain it, the more unstable it becomes. If we lower the power to reduce instability, the bridge collapses too quickly to be useful."

"So, we're walking a tightrope," Ted observed. "Too much power, and it destabilises; too little, and it fails."

"Precisely," Zach replied. "Our challenge is to find a way to maintain stability without increasing power—or to manage the instabilities in a way that doesn't harm what we send through."

"Have you tried alternative methods to reinforce the bridge?" Ted asked.

"I'm exploring a few options," Zach said, gesturing to the schematics on his workstation. "One idea is to enhance the efficiency of the quantum entanglement capacitor. If we can optimise how the flux interacts, we might achieve stability at lower energy levels."

Ted's eyes scanned the diagrams. "That could be the breakthrough we need. But we have to move swiftly. The board is eager for results."

"I understand," Zach said, the expectation clear. "I'm confident we're close. With some adjustments, we can prepare for a full-scale test."

"Good," Ted said, his gaze steady. "But remember, Zach, this technology has far-reaching implications. It's not just about scientific achievement; it's about how we shape the future."

Zach nodded. "I know. We have a responsibility to ensure it's used ethically."

"Especially with competitors like Obsidian Industries hard on our heels." Ted cautioned. "We can't afford any missteps or leaks."

"I've tightened our security protocols," Zach assured him. "Our work stays within these walls."

"See that it does," Ted replied. "Now, show me your latest findings."

Zach led Ted through his recent experiments, highlighting the progress and the hurdles. "We've managed to reduce the aging effect slightly by tweaking the temporal harmonics," he explained. "It's not a complete fix, but it's a step in the right direction."

"What about inanimate objects?" Ted asked. "Do they experience any temporal anomalies?"

"Interestingly, they remain unaffected," Zach said. "It's the complexity of living organisms that complicates things."

"Perhaps we need to isolate biological samples from temporal influence," Ted suggested.

"That's one of the strategies I'm pursuing," Zach replied. "If we can create a protective field around the biological matter during transit, we might shield it from the distortions."

"Keep at it," he encouraged. "This could everything."

As Ted prepared to leave, he placed a reassuring hand on Zach's arm. "You're doing remarkable work. We're counting on you."

"Thank you," Zach said sincerely. "I won't let us down."

After Ted exited, Zach returned to the prototype, his mind racing with possibilities. The Quantum Bridge wasn't just a scientific marvel—it was a gateway to a new era. The potential applications were staggering, instant global connectivity, travel to other places, perhaps even other times.

He contemplated the societal impact, and the potential applications were nothing short of staggering. The barriers of distance would crumble. Humanitarian aid could reach disaster zones the moment catastrophe struck, saving countless lives. Critical resources like vaccines and medications could be dispatched globally without delay,

The possibilities stretched even further. The bridge could enable exploration of the furthest galaxies without the constraints of conventional space travel. Scientists could step onto distant planets, accelerating our understanding of the universe exponentially.

And if the bridge could manipulate temporal dimensions—as some theoretical models suggested—the implications were even more profound. Time itself could become a navigable dimension. Historians might witness pivotal moments in human history firsthand, learning truths lost to the ages.

But he was also acutely aware of the risks. Such power could be misused if it fell into the wrong hands—used for coercion, control, or worse. It was up to him and his team to navigate these ethical waters carefully.

Turning back to the control panel, a new idea sparked. "What if we adjust the synchronization of the quantum states?" he mused to himself. "By fine-tuning the alignment, maybe we can enhance stability without upping the power."

He began inputting new parameters, his fingers flying over the keyboard. The prototype hummed softly, its inner workings a dance of particles and energy beyond visible sight. As he initiated the test, the device emitted a gentle glow, and the air around it seemed to shimmer subtly.

Data streamed across the monitors, and Zach's heart leaped. The stability readings were better than ever, and the temporal distortion on the test sample had decreased significantly.

"This is it," he whispered, excitement surging through him. "We're getting there."

He leaned back, allowing himself a moment to relish the breakthrough. It wasn't the final answer, but it was a significant leap forward. The bridge was becoming more than a theoretical construct—it was edging closer to practical reality.

As he began shutting down the equipment for the night, Zach felt exhilarated. The Quantum Bridge held the promise of transforming the world, and he was at the helm of this extraordinary adventure.

With great innovation came great responsibility. He was not just building a machine; he was shaping the future. The ethical considerations loomed large, and he knew he had to tread carefully.

Locking up the lab, Zach stepped into the night. The future awaited, and he was poised to meet it.

There was no turning back now.

05 – DAVINA'S GAME

*"It's not power that corrupts but the
fear of losing it that does."*

Obsidian Industries, The Tower, 1 St. George Wharf, Vauxhall, London SW8 2DA – 09:58 AM, February 19

Davina Drake stepped gracefully out of the sleek black limousine that had pulled up before the towering edifice. The chauffeur scarcely had time to open her door before she glided through the glass entrance of The Tower, headquarters of Obsidian Industries. The clock displayed a little before ten in the morning—punctuality was a concern for lesser mortals. Davina moved at her own pace, every step deliberate, calculated.

"Good morning, ma'am," came the chorus from staff as she passed through the atrium, a few heads dipping slightly out of habit rather than necessity. She offered no response beyond a fleeting glance, making her way to the private lift that would whisk her to the executive floor.

The lift doors opened directly into her office on the ninety-ninth floor. The air inside was cool and pristine, the subtle scent of fresh flowers ever-present. Floor-to-ceiling windows offered sweeping views over Vauxhall

Cross, a perfect backdrop befitting her status. Davina chose not to sit. She preferred to pause at this hour, taking in the expanse of the Thames below. Power, she often mused, was best appreciated from a height.

She stood majestic in the centre of her palatial office, lights dimmed to cast long shadows across sleek, state-of-the-art furnishings. Rain caressed the vast windows, a soft, rhythmic backdrop to her thoughts. Taking in the view, her fingers lightly traced the glass as she observed the microscopic world below. Everything and everyone seemed so small from up here, so insignificant. But Davina didn't feel small. Not anymore.

Her reflection stared back—poised, controlled, with a fire burning bright. Outwardly, she embodied success—polished, accomplished, untouchable. And those who underestimated her soon discovered there was far more to Davina Drake than met the eye.

Obsidian Industries had granted her power and influence, but it was not enough. Not yet. The project was the key—an opportunity to transcend the boundaries of time and reality itself. She had no intention of sharing that power, especially not with the faceless bureaucrats funding the research.

A sharp knock interrupted her reverie. Without waiting for permission, her personal assistant, Natalie Blake, entered—a vision of cold professionalism in a pinstriped suit. Attractive in a severe way, Natalie's expression was perpetually that of someone who had just tasted something sour.

"Your coffee, Ms. Drake," Natalie announced, placing the cup on the desk with military precision. "Your first meeting is at eleven o'clock with Ted Barker from Daystrom. Shall I run through your agenda for the day?"

Davina nodded, her eyes still scanning the city-scape. "Proceed."

Natalie flipped open her tablet, reciting a list of appointments. Davina listened absently—meetings, presentations, status updates. Necessary formalities. But when Natalie mentioned Subject Mondori, her attention sharpened.

"Ted Barker will brief you on the latest data regarding the subject at eleven. Shall I confirm the meeting?"

Finally taking her seat, Davina's perfectly manicured fingers grazed the surface of the desk. "Yes. And Natalie—ensure Barker has everything he requires. He's crucial at this stage of our plans."

"Of course, Ms. Drake," Natalie replied, though there was the faintest hint of sarcasm in her tone as she departed. Some people clung to small rebellions. Davina had no patience for it. The world offered no mercy for hesitation, no place for the fragile. She would ensure that Natalie's defiance was addressed. She demanded unwavering obedience from her team.

A soft chime sounded from her desk. Crossing the room, she glanced at the screen—a message from one of her contacts, confirming that her latest intervention had yielded results. A slow, calculated smile formed, never quite reaching her eyes.

Ted was becoming a problem—an obstacle. He knew more than he admitted, and his secrecy rendered him a liability. Davina understood that information was the most valuable currency, and Ted was withholding some of it. That would need to change.

As the clock edged toward eleven, Ted Barker arrived precisely on time, empty-handed as per security protocol when meeting senior executives. She greeted him with the same polished grace she extended to all corporate partners, making him feel like the most significant person in the room. The meeting was swift—the usual updates, including progress on the Quantum Bridge.

Once Ted had departed, she waited a moment before picking up her phone, dialling a number known only to a select few. "Instruct Mikhail to keep a close watch on both Barker and Mondori," she commanded. "They're withholding information. If they don't start cooperating... ensure Mikhail follows up."

She reviewed the latest report—a visit to Mondori's residence. Turning over the pieces of the puzzle she'd been assembling for months, Davina contemplated her next move. The Daystrom Institute had long been on her radar, but Mondori's research had truly captured her interest. A method to control the fabric of reality, to manipulate time itself. It was more than mere science—it was ultimate power. And she intended to claim it.

Davina had been scrutinizing Ted closely. Gaps in the data had become apparent, inconsistencies that didn't align. For all his professionalism, Ted was hiding something. She could sense it. But patience was a virtue she possessed in abundance. One way or another, she always got what she wanted.

A knock at the door pulled her from her thoughts.

"Come."

One of her associates stepped in—a tall, thin man with dark hair and a perpetually anxious demeanour. Clutching a folder, his eyes avoided hers, darting nervously around the room.

"Davina," he began hesitantly, "I have the additional information you requested on the Keane's."

Her smile returned, small and predatory. "Excellent. Leave it on my desk."

He nodded, placing the folder before her. "One more thing. She was seen alone with Dr. Mondori at the recent Sky Garden event."

Her painted fingernails grazed the folder's edge. "Very good, Marcus. Continue monitoring her. Inform me immediately of any unusual developments."

Marcus nodded swiftly and exited, leaving her alone once more. Opening the folder, she skimmed through reports, surveillance logs, transcripts. If she could control the Bridge and harness its power, she could rewrite the rules of existence. And there was something far more personal at stake, something that couldn't be undone by any other means.

Her thoughts shifted to Isabella Keane and, in particular, her husband, James. He was useful in more ways than one. His guilt and vulnerability made him easy to manipulate. Clinging to the remnants of a failing marriage, grasping at a life slipping away—the cracks were evident. And his wandering attention towards attractive women made him an ideal pawn, ready to fall completely under her influence.

But James wasn't the only piece in play.

Isabella intrigued her. There was something about her, the way she moved, how she spoke. A secret waiting to be exposed. With her estranged husband a part of the equation, the opportunities for exploitation abounded.

Crossing to the bar, Davina poured herself a vodka, contemplating her strategy. Coffee was for the uninspired. Ted wouldn't break easily, but everyone had a tipping point. And Isabella? Perhaps her marriage was her Achilles' heel. Davina had witnessed how people's carefully constructed lives crumbled when fractures appeared. It wouldn't take much to push her over the edge, to make her question everything she believed.

She savoured the sharpness of the drink, the warmth spreading as she devised her next move. Precision and caution were essential, but she had never shied away from risk. The rewards promised were too great.

A call from one of her executive assistants interrupted her musings—a reminder about the upcoming meeting with the board. Those men were so predictable, fixated on bottom lines and quarterly figures. They failed to grasp the grander vision, the true magnitude of what was at stake. But she did.

Ending the call, her resolve hardened. The board's power plays were inconsequential if she controlled the technology. And she would. It was merely a matter of time.

Returning to her desk, she gazed out over the city once more. The rain blurred the outlines of buildings, making the world below seem fluid, malleable. Just like reality itself could be, in the right hands. Her hands.

***

Davina Drake's penthouse, Wellington House, 67 Vincent Square, Westminster, London SW1P 2PA - 10:30 PM, February 19

Later that evening, Davina found herself standing atop the rooftop terrace of her penthouse, the wind teasing strands of her hair as she gazed over the sprawling cityscape. The rain had ceased, leaving the world beneath her glistening under the glow of streetlamps. Up here, the city felt distant, the cacophony of urban life muted. She relished these moments—alone with her thoughts and meticulously crafted plans.

Her mind drifted once more to James Keane. It would be effortless to sow seeds of doubt within him, to make him question the life he had built with Isabella. He was already teetering on the brink; a gentle nudge would suffice to tip him over. And she would catch him when he fell, steering him toward a future aligned with her ambitions.

Davina inhaled deeply, the crisp evening air filling her lungs as she allowed herself a rare moment of introspection. The Quantum Bridge was the linchpin—it always had been. She was perhaps the only one who truly grasped its limitless potential.

But now, it was getting late.

She returned indoors, the glass panel closing behind her. She took a lazy stroll, vodka glass in hand, to the bedroom. There, her chosen companion—her toy for the night—waited patiently, ready to play his part.

She had a final task to attend to before retiring for the evening. A stream of shower water rinsed away the tension of the day, cleaning her body if not her soul. This was her sanctuary, her safe haven.

Later, as she lay there, her companion spent, she looked out into the night, the stars stretching infinitely above, each one a beacon of possibility. She envisioned it all with crystal clarity—how every piece on the chessboard would serve her strategy, how each calculated move would draw her closer to the power she deserved.

She had learned the rules of the game through hardship and determination.

Whatever the game, Davina always came out on top.

06 – AN UNEXPECTED INTERVIEW

"It's often the unseen hands that weave the threads of fate."

Daystrom Institute, Level 77, Meridian Tower, 12 Meridian Place, Canary Wharf, London - *10:55 AM, February 20*

Maggie stepped out of the black London cab that had just eased to a stop outside the Daystrom Institute. The car melded back into the flow of morning traffic as she paused to take in the towering glass and steel structure before her. The Institute was a marvel of modern architecture—gleaming surfaces reflecting the sunlight, a vast atrium filled with natural light, and an atmosphere buzzing with purpose. It was a place where grand ideas took shape, where innovation met precision.

As she crossed the lobby, scientists, engineers, and corporate professionals moved with determined strides —engaged in animated discussions, hurrying to meetings, or savouring a quick coffee from the café nestled in a corner. Maggie's presence drew a few curious glances; she wore no badge, carried no briefcase, yet exuded an air of confidence that suggested she belonged.

At the reception desk, a courteous attendant greeted her. "Good morning, may I assist you?"

"Maggie Carter. I have an appointment with Ted Barker," she replied, offering a curious smile that hinted at both openness and mystery.

The receptionist tapped a few keys, scanning the schedule. "Yes, Ms. Carter, you're expected. Mr. Barker's office is on the seventy-seventh floor. The lifts are just to your left."

"Thank you," she said, heading toward the lifts without hesitation.

Ted Barker's office was a blend of modern elegance and understated authority. Her office affording a panoramic view, the urban canvas laid out beneath a clear blue sky. As she entered, Ted stood behind his desk, glancing up from a report. In his fifties, with neatly styled silver hair and sharp eyes, he carried himself with the assurance of someone accustomed to being the most knowledgeable person in the room.

"Ms. Carter," Ted began, extending his hand.

"Please, call me Maggie," she said, shaking his hand firmly.

"Very well, Maggie," he replied, openly revealing his curiosity. "I assume you're here for the grand tour."

She smiled softly. "That would be wonderful."

He gestured toward the corridor. "Shall we? I must admit, several colleagues of mine were quite impressed by you at the gala, yet I couldn't find much about your professional background."

As they walked, she gaze took in every detail. "I prefer to keep a low profile. I've found that meaningful work often happens away from the spotlight."

Ted glanced at her, intrigued. "In our field, most are eager to showcase their achievements. Why the discretion?"

She met his eyes briefly. "Those who need to know, do. For the rest, I let my work speak for itself when the time is right."

A subtle smile played on Ted's lips. "An interesting approach. May I ask which organisation you represent? Obsidian Industries, perhaps? Or one of our international *counterparts*?"

"I'm an independent consultant," Maggie replied smoothly. "I collaborate with teams on complex projects that require a... unique perspective."

They reached a viewing window overlooking one of the Institute's state-of-the-art laboratories. Scientists in white coats moved with focused intent, huddled over glowing screens and intricate equipment.

"What brings you to Daystrom specifically?" Ted asked, his curiosity growing.

Her eyes lingered on the lab below. "I'm particularly interested in your Quantum Bridge project."

He raised an eyebrow. "Not many outside this building are aware of the details of that initiative."

She turned, her expression composed. "I've made it a point to stay informed about cutting-edge research in quantum mechanics. Your team's work is groundbreaking."

He studied her carefully. "We have made significant progress, transmitting cellular material across the bridge and retrieving it. However, we're facing challenges with time distortion causing cellular aging. Reversing that effect has been… elusive."

She nodded thoughtfully. "And the variances you've encountered—those must be complicating matters."

His gaze sharpened. "Variances?"

She continued calmly. "The fluctuations in bridge stability correlated with power input. Lowering the power reduces these variances but causes the bridge to collapse prematurely. At higher power levels, the bridge endures but becomes unstable."

He regarded her with equal parts of surprise and caution. "You're remarkably well-informed for an independent consultant."

Her smile was encouraging. "I've encountered similar phenomena in previous projects. The challenges you're facing aren't entirely unexpected given the parameters of quantum entanglement and temporal distortion."

Ted folded his arms, intrigued despite himself. "Do you have any suggestions on how to address these variances?"

Maggie leaned slightly against the railing, her gaze distant as she gathered her thoughts. "Have you considered that the issue isn't solely about power levels, but about resonance? Instead of forcing stability through increased power, perhaps aligning the bridge's frequency with the temporal fluctuations could create a harmonious equilibrium."

He pondered her words. "You're suggesting we adjust the bridge's parameters to synchronise with the inherent temporal variances?"

"Exactly," she affirmed. "By achieving resonance, you may stabilise the bridge without the need for excessive power, thereby minimising the aging effect on biological samples."

Ted paused, processing the implications. "It's an intriguing theory. We've been so focused on counteracting the variances that we haven't explored harmonizing with them."

She glanced at him, her eyes expressing the depth of her understanding. "Sometimes the solution isn't to oppose the forces at play, but to move in concert with them."

He felt a stir of excitement mixed with caution. "Your insights could be invaluable. May I ask where you've applied these concepts before?"

"In various capacities," she replied, her tone gently evasive. "I've worked on projects involving quantum field stabilization and multiverse theories. Each presented unique challenges, but the underlying principles often intersect."

Ted nodded slowly. "Your expertise is evident, yet I find it curious that someone with your knowledge isn't affiliated with any known institution."

She smiled lightly. "As I said, I prefer to operate independently. It allows me the freedom to engage with projects that truly captivate me."

They continued down the corridor, passing displays of the Institute's achievements. Ted sensed there was more to Maggie than met the eye, but he couldn't deny the potential value of her perspective.

"Would you be interested in consulting with our team?" he asked, glancing at her.

"I would," she replied without hesitation. "On the condition that I can work closely with your lead scientist. Zach Mondori, isn't it?"

"Yes, Zach is heading the project," he confirmed. "He's been instrumental in bringing the Quantum Bridge to its current stage."

"I believe our collaboration could accelerate your progress," she responded confidently. "I have some ideas that might help address the challenges you're facing."

Ted considered her proposal. Trust didn't come easily in his line of work, but her knowledge was compelling. "Very well. I'll arrange for you to meet with Zach and the team. We'll need you to sign a confidentiality agreement, of course."

"Naturally," she agreed.

They paused outside Ted's office, the tour having come full circle. He extended his hand once more. "Welcome aboard, Maggie. I look forward to seeing what you bring to the table."

She shook his hand firmly. "Thank you, Ted. I appreciate

the opportunity."

As she departed, he watched her leave with a degree of caution. There was an air of enigma about her, a sense that she was playing a game whose rules only she understood. But in the high-stakes world of quantum research, sometimes it took an unconventional mind to unlock the next breakthrough.

She headed back through the bustling lobby, private conversations and purposeful footsteps filling the air. Stepping outside, she paused to glance back at the imposing structure of the Daystrom Institute. A flicker of a smile touched her lips before she disappeared, blending seamlessly with the flow of the city.

Little did they know what the future held in store for them.

07 – TEMPTING FATE

"Often, the truest selves are hidden behind the masks we present to the world."

Hotel Napoleon, Boulevard de Waterloo 33, 1000 Brussels – *08:00 PM, February 20*

The back seat of the cab ought to have been a sanctuary, a place to unwind, yet James Keane found himself unable to find solace. The rain-soaked streets of Brussels blurred into a dreary tangle behind the window, mirroring his mood. Pedestrians huddled under umbrellas, cyclists splashed through puddles, but he didn't even register their presence. His mind drifted hundreds of miles away—to London, to the home where tension had gathered like storm clouds and now finally unleashed its tempest.

He sighed deeply, sinking further into the seat, fingers absently tracing the smooth screen of his buzzing phone. Another message. Another meeting. Once, his work had been a sanctuary, a distraction from the widening chasm between him and Isabella. Now, it felt like the very force pulling him under, tightening its grasp around his life.

Family.

The word felt hollow, a formality uttered without conviction. When was the last time they had spoken without an argument simmering beneath their words? When had they shared a meal without the oppressive silence stretching between them, as if they had forgotten how to be together?

He cradled his head in his hands, the memory of their most recent argument flashing vividly. She had confronted him again about his long hours, his growing detachment. But what could he say? Work had become his alibi, the sole anchor in his drifting existence. Deadlines, projects, relentless demands—it was all a façade, wasn't it? The more he immersed himself in work, the more his life seemed to unravel.

She was no longer the woman he had married. The warmth and connection they once cherished had faded. In their place stood someone cool, distant—a stranger. And Katie... their daughter, once his confidante, had become remote as well, her rebelliousness a constant reminder that he was losing his grip on everything that mattered.

His phone buzzed again. Still no reply from Isabella. Only silence. The meeting had overrun, and now, even the thought of hurrying to the airport felt futile.

The taxi pulled up outside the hotel, and he paid the fare, stepping out into the downpour. Rain soaked through his jacket, but he scarcely felt it, ensnared in a spiral of guilt and frustration. He needed to mend things, to return to the life they once shared before it all began to crumble.

The hotel lobby greeted him with sterile indifference—gleaming floors, muted tones, and a hint of artificial freshness. It felt as empty as the house awaiting him in London. He sank into his bed, his phone buzzing once more. This time, it wasn't a work email. It was Davina.

He hesitated, thumb hovering over the screen. Davina Drake. A business associate from Obsidian Industries, one of several companies linked to his consultancy work. What had begun as professional dialogue had recently taken on a different undertone.

You're in Brussels, right? Me too. Thought we could catch up—discuss the latest.

Davina rarely wasted time on pleasantries. She was direct, incisive. Yet beneath her cool confidence lurked something else—a restlessness he recognised within himself. He considered ignoring the message but found himself typing a reply instead.

Yes, still here. Free for a bit if you'd like to meet.

Within minutes, they arranged to meet at a quiet bar nearby. As he changed out of his rain-soaked clothes, unease hanging over him. This was merely business, nothing more. He descended the dimly lit corridor, a cocktail of guilt and alcohol fuelling his mind.

The bar was cloaked in soft shadows, a soothing backdrop to the rain-slicked streets beyond. Davina was already there, seated at a secluded table, her glass of wine catching the dim light. She smiled as he approached, and something tightened within him. Her smile was always the same—sharp, alluring, with a touch of mystery, as if she knew more than she let on.

"James," she greeted warmly as he took his seat. "Glad you could make it."

He nodded, attempting a smile. "Thought we might as well catch up. Business is business."

Her eyes glinted. "Yes, of course. I've been meaning to discuss a few matters—business-related, naturally."

The subtle inflection in her voice suggested this wasn't solely about work.

Their conversation ebbed and flowed, drifting from professional topics into more personal realms. She had a knack for drawing him out, coaxing him to share thoughts he hadn't voiced to anyone else—his frustrations, his doubts, his marriage. For reasons he couldn't fully comprehend, he opened up, revealing more than he'd intended.

"You seem tense," Davina observed, her gaze both sharp and sympathetic. "Is everything all right at home?"

He stiffened, her question hitting too close to the mark. "It's fine. Just... busy."

"Busy or complicated?" Her tone softened, carrying a note of understanding that unsettled him.

He hesitated, but the words slipped out before he could stop them. "Complicated," he admitted. "Isabella and I... things haven't been the same for a while. It's been difficult."

Davina leaned back, crossing her legs, watching him with a contemplative gaze, as if calculating her next move.

"Sometimes," she mused, "we stay in situations that no longer work simply because they're familiar. Even if they're suffocating us."

Her words struck deep. He had clung to routine out of habit. But was it comforting anymore? Or merely... there?

"I suppose," he murmured, staring into his drink.

She leaned forward, her voice lowering. "You deserve more than just going through the motions, James."

A flush of emotion rose within him, a mixture of guilt and something else twisting inside. Her words were tempting, her presence magnetic. She offered an escape from the monotony. But it came at a price—he sensed it, even if he couldn't name it.

"What are you implying?" he asked, meeting her gaze.

She smiled seductively, a scent of desire in every word she spoke. "I'm suggesting you don't have to remain trapped in a place that's holding you back. There are other possibilities—other paths."

Her words were laced with innuendo. The boundary between professional and personal blurred, and he wasn't certain what she was offering. But the way she looked at him, how her gaze lingered—it was evident she wasn't solely discussing business.

Guilt tugged at him, but recklessness always won. He'd spent his life pretending to do the right thing, to be loyal, but he knew how far he was from that truth. And now, in this moment, Davina was offering him something different.

"You don't understand my situation," he said, resorting to his often-used excuse to justify his indiscretions.

Her smile deepened, eyes gleaming. "How many times have you used that excuse, James? I know so much more about you than you realise."

"She knew about his marital troubles, his frustrations with work and life, and his extramarital affairs. She was after something, and she was pulling him into it.

He took a steadying breath. "What is it you're after, Davina?"

Her smile faded, replaced by a serious expression. "I'm simply ensuring that golden opportunities aren't missed. And James... you're standing on the brink of one right now."

Her words were both a warning and a temptation. She was offering him a way out, a new direction—but it would undoubtedly come at a cost.

He stood up abruptly, his thoughts in turmoil. He needed to get out of there, to clear his head. But as he turned, Davina moved swiftly, her leg brushing against his beneath the table. Without giving him time to react, she reached out and grasped his tie firmly, yanking him back toward her.

Their faces were suddenly close—too close. The heat of her sigh brushing against him. He felt the sharp tension between them, an undeniable electricity coursing through the air.

Her lips hovered near his ear, a voice like smooth velvet. "Think about what I've said, James. You don't have to be trapped. You can choose another path. It seems to me your wife is already doing that—or did you not notice how she looked at Zach Mondori the other night?"

Her words overwhelmed him. Then, with a sudden release, she let go of his tie, the fabric slipping through her fingers like an unspoken farewell. He stood there, conflicted, caught between guilt and the temptation she had ignited.

He exited the bar, stepping into the rain-soaked night, her words echoing in his mind. As he walked back to the hotel, hands shoved into his pockets, turmoil wrestled with desire.

Back in his room, he collapsed onto the bed, staring up at the ceiling. His phone lay silent beside him—no messages from Isabella, no one waiting for him at home.

He wasn't sure he wanted to return home.

08 – FOLDS IN THE FABRIC

"Of all the words of mice and men, the saddest are, 'It might have been.'"

The Daystrom Institute, Level 22, Meridian Tower 12 Meridian Place Canary Wharf, London E14 9PL - 02:00 PM, February 24

Maggie approached the laboratory. Her first day of work. Again.

Technicians hovered over expensive consoles, their faces illuminated by the glow of complex data streams dancing across the monitors. The room hummed with energy, dominated by a large, circular platform at its centre. Resting upon it was the Quantum Bridge prototype—silent, imposing, like a slumbering giant awaiting its moment.

Zach looked up as she approached, removing his protective goggles. The recognition of a friendly face softened his typically intense expression. "Maggie," he greeted. "Right on time. We're about to initiate the first test of the full-scale prototype. I'm glad you're here."

She returned his smile, though a whisper of something unreadable passed through her eyes. "I wouldn't miss this for the world. After all, I'm here to help, aren't I?"

He gestured toward the apparatus. "Scaling up from the desktop model is a significant leap. I've conducted countless tests on the smaller version, but this... this is uncharted territory."

She stepped closer, her focus on the intricate web of circuitry and components. "You've done excellent work with the interface. However..." She trailed off, her fingers lightly tracing a series of cables. "Have you accounted for potential quantum feedback loops in this circuit? At this scale, you might not just create a bridge—you could inadvertently distort the local quantum field."

Zach blinked, momentarily caught off guard. "Quantum feedback loops? I've read about them, but I didn't think —"

"It's a subtle effect," she interjected gently. "But if you calibrate the phase variances here"—she pointed to a cluster of nodes—"you should be able to minimise any unwanted feedback."

He studied the area she highlighted, admiration mingling with surprise. "That's impressive. I hadn't considered it from that angle. I've been focusing on stabilizing temporal shifts, but feedback loops weren't on my radar yet."

She offered a modest shrug, her gaze steady. "Just a thought. Similar issues arise in high-energy quantum systems I've worked with before."

Turning to face her fully, Zach's eyes held a newfound respect. "I'd be interested to hear more about your experience with other quantum systems. Perhaps over lunch?"

Maggie hesitated briefly before nodding. "Certainly. I know a café near Kensington Gardens you might like."

A genuine smile spread across his face. "La Dolce Vita? That's one of my favourite spots. Tomorrow, then?"

"Tomorrow," she agreed, a subtle warmth touching her expression as she returned her attention to the console.

***

A short while later, the team was engrossed in the intricate dance of numbers and waveforms flickering across their screens. The hum from the Quantum Bridge device grew louder as the coils energised, the air tingling with static electricity.

"Ready for the first test," Zach announced, his excitement barely contained. His hands hovered over the activation panel as he surveyed the room. Team members signalled their readiness with nods and focused gazes.

Just as he was about to power up the prototype, the door

swung open. Ted Barker entered with his customary aura of authority, now edged with urgency. Without preamble, he headed straight over.

"Zach, a word?" His tone was firm but low.

Zach straightened, stepping away from the controls. "What's going on?"

Ted glanced around before speaking. "The board wants to accelerate the test phase."

A furrow formed between Zach's brows. "Accelerate? We've not completed this stage. We can't move any faster than we're doing; not without opening ourselves us to unacceptable risks."

"I know," Ted replied, his eyes steady. "But they're feeling the pressure. Certain competitors are becoming more aggressive. If we don't push forward, someone else will."

Zach's gaze shifted to Maggie, who watched them with composed interest, then back to Ted. "We can't rush this. The variances in the data remain an issue. If we're not cautious, we could compromise everything."

Ted rested a hand on his shoulder. "That's why I've proposed shifts—you, me, and Maggie. One of us will always be here to oversee the process."

He sighed, weighing the proposal. "All right. But I

need to be informed immediately of any anomalies or deviations."

"Agreed," Ted said. He turned to address the team, his authority carrying through. "Listen up, everyone. The board has decided to expedite our schedule. Effective immediately, we'll be working around the clock. I know it's a significant demand, but we're so close now. Your dedication is crucial."

A ripple of murmurs spread through the room, a mix of apprehension and anticipation. Zach returned to the console, his resolve firming. "Let's proceed, then."

With a decisive motion, he activated the prototype. The room dimmed slightly as the Quantum Bridge powered up, the machinery emitting a deep hum that resonated through the floor.

"Phase one holding steady," an assistant called out. "Initiating phase two ramp-up."

As the power intensified, Maggie felt a wave of confusion wash over her. The edges of her vision blurred, and a strange dissonance filled her senses. It was as if the world had shifted, leaving her momentarily unmoored. She gripped a nearby chair, trying to steady herself.

"Maggie?" Zach's voice sounded distant, muffled by the pounding in her ears. "We're getting promising data. Almost ready to proceed to phase three."

She forced herself to respond, her voice merely a fraction above a whisper. "I... I need a moment."

Without waiting for a reply, she turned and made her way out of the lab, her pass unsteady. The corridor seemed to stretch before her, each step echoing unnaturally. She reached the restroom and slipped inside, locking the door behind her. Leaning over the sink, she splashed cold water on her face, willing the unsettling sensations to pass.

Staring into the mirror, she barely recognised the pallor of her reflection. For a second it seemed as though another face flickered beside her own—a shadow of someone she used to be. Shaking her head, she tightened her eyes, taking slow, measured breaths until the world righted itself.

Gathering herself, she smoothed her hair and straightened her blouse. Whatever was happening, she couldn't afford to let it interfere. Not now.

Back in the lab, the team remained engrossed in the test. Maggie re-entered quietly, taking her place without drawing attention. Zach glanced her way, concern flickering in his eyes. She offered a reassuring nod, and he returned his focus to the task at hand.

***

Several floors below, in the isolation ward, Isabella moved methodically from one patient to the next. The room was tranquil, filled with the soft hum of equipment and the gentle murmur of her colleagues. The day's final round of tests was proceeding smoothly.

As she checked a patient's chart, she noticed his gaze had grown distant, eyes unfocused. "Mr. Thompson?" she asked softly, but he didn't respond.

"Isabella," Sarah called from her post, her voice tinged with alarm. "Something's wrong here."

Turning, Isabella saw that all the patients were exhibiting the same vacant stare, their expressions blank. She shuddered. "What's happening?"

Other team members exchanged anxious glances. "They're unresponsive," one nurse reported. "Vitals are normal, but it's like they're… not here."

Isabella moved swiftly between patients, checking pulses and pupil responses. "This can't be a coincidence," she murmured. "All of them at once?"

"Should we call for medical assistance?" Sarah asked, her eyes wide with concern.

"Not yet," Isabella replied, her mind racing. "Let's monitor them closely and document everything."

Minutes stretched on, heavy with tension. Then, as suddenly as it began, the patients started to stir. Blinks, faint movements, a gradual return of awareness. They appeared disoriented but unharmed.

Relief mingled with confusion. "Let's run full evaluations," Isabella instructed. "I want detailed reports on each patient."

As the team moved to comply, she couldn't stop thinking that something profound had just occurred. The simultaneous nature of the episode defied explanation. Her thoughts drifted to the experimental treatments, searching for a link.

"Isabella," Sarah whispered, drawing her aside. "What do you think caused that? I've never seen anything this severe before."

She met her colleague's gaze, uncertainty knotting in her stomach. "I don't know," she admitted. "But we're going to find out."

Deep down, a nagging suspicion took root. This was more than a medical anomaly. Something larger was at play, threads weaving together in ways she couldn't yet comprehend.

Looking back at the patients, now engaging quietly with the staff, Isabella resolved to uncover the truth. The question echoed in her mind: They all experienced the same episode at the same moment.

How unlikely was that?

09 – A SLIGHT OF HAND

"Sometimes what appears as an accident is merely destiny's hand guiding us toward a greater good."

The Daystrom Institute, Level 75, Meridian Tower, 12 Meridian Place, Canary Wharf, London – *7:42 AM, February 25*

Isabella adjusted her face mask and meticulously fine-tuned the centrifuge settings. Her research demanded precision, and the rhythmic routine of analysis, testing, and retesting had brought order to her thoughts. The laboratory's soft hum enveloped her, a familiar symphony that usually helped her focus.

But today, her thoughts were scattered like leaves in the wind. The patients had all experienced a simultaneous, inexplicable episode—a drift into a dreamlike state that defied any logical explanation. She had reviewed the dosages administered; everything was identical to previous treatments. No anomalies, no deviations. Yet something was amiss.

She willed herself to concentrate. As she reached for a vial from the storage unit, the overhead lights flickered briefly. Isabella glanced up, a wisp of unease tightening within her. The power fluctuations were becoming more frequent; she made a mental note to report them to maintenance. Shaking off the momentary distraction, she reminded herself that fatigue was likely playing tricks on her. The long hours, the mounting pressure from the board, and James's recent outburst were all taking their toll.

Her fingers wrapped around the cool glass of the vial when the sound of footsteps echoed behind her. Startled, she turned to see Maggie standing at the doorway.

"Maggie?" Isabella said, surprised. "I didn't expect anyone else to be here this late."

Maggie returned a teasing smile. "I was looking for Zach. Have you seen him?"

Isabella shook her head. "Not since the gala. He's been putting in long hours, though. Maybe he left already."

"Perhaps," Maggie replied, stepping further into the lab. Her gaze wandered over the array of instruments and chemicals. "You're burning the midnight oil too, I see. Working on something interesting?"

Isabella hesitated, unsure how much to share. Her work was confidential, but Maggie's approachable demeanour put her at ease. "It's... complicated," she began. "My patients experienced a strange episode today. They all slipped into some kind of trance at the same time, but I can't find any reason why."

Maggie moved closer, her expression thoughtful. "That does sound perplexing. Do you think it might be related to quantum entanglement?"

"Quantum entanglement?" Isabella echoed, her eyebrows knitting in confusion. "That's not really my area. I'm focusing on biochemical responses."

"True," Maggie acknowledged, "but quantum phenomena can sometimes manifest in unexpected ways, especially in complex systems like the human brain. Emotions and consciousness might interact with quantum states more than we realise."

Isabella pondered her words, a spark of intrigue igniting. The idea seemed far-fetched, yet strangely plausible. Could there be an unseen connection influencing her patients?

"Maybe," she conceded. "It's an angle I hadn't considered."

Her colleague offered an encouraging smile. "Sometimes looking beyond our usual parameters can shed new light on a problem. If you'd like, I could help you explore this. Perhaps there's an overlap with some of Zach's work."

Isabella felt a mixture of gratitude and hesitation. Maggie's sudden interest was unexpected, but her insight was valuable. "I suppose a fresh perspective couldn't hurt," she admitted.

As she reached for the vial, ready to continue her work, Maggie stepped forward to point at something on the lab table. Their movements intersected, and Maggie's elbow gently bumped Isabella's arm. The vial slipped from her fingers, the liquid spilling onto her skin.

"Oh!" Isabella gasped, quickly setting the vial down. A tingling sensation spread across her hand, warm and unsettling.

Maggie's eyes widened. "I'm so sorry! Are you okay?" She glanced at her own arm, brushing her sleeve as if checking for spills. "Did any get on me?"

Isabella grabbed a cloth, wiping her hand as the warmth began to fade. "I think I'm fine. It's just a mild reagent, but I should probably wash it off."

"Let me help," Maggie said, her tone sounded sincere. She handed Isabella a fresh cloth, her gaze attentive. "These things happen in the lab all the time, don't they?"

"Yes, accidents occur," Isabella agreed, though a subtle unease lingered. The incident felt odd, but she couldn't pinpoint why.

Maggie dabbed at her sleeve, then gave a light laugh. "Looks like I escaped unscathed. Still, better safe than sorry."

Isabella managed a small smile. "Thank you. I appreciate your concern."

"Of course," she replied, her eyes meeting Isabella's. "And about earlier—I didn't mean to intrude. I genuinely think we might find some answers together."

"Perhaps," Isabella said softly. The warmth in her hand had subsided, leaving only a faint tingling. "It's worth exploring."

"Great," she said, her enthusiasm returning. "Actually, I was thinking—we both could use a break. How about coffee tomorrow? There's a charming café near Kensington Gardens called La Dolce Vita. It's the perfect place to clear our heads."

Isabella hesitated, her responsibilities pressing against the idea of taking time away. Yet the thought of a peaceful moment of respite, away from the stresses of home and work, was undeniably appealing.

"That sounds nice," she found herself saying. "Midday?"

"Perfect," Maggie agreed, her smile brightening. "It's a date. Well, not a date, but you know what I mean."

Isabella chuckled lightly. "I do."

Maggie gathered her bag, her movements graceful. "I should let you get back to it. And again, I'm sorry about the spill."

"Don't worry about it," Isabella reassured her. "I'll see you tomorrow."

As her colleague left the lab, the door closing softly behind her, Isabella took stock of her surroundings. The room felt different now—quieter, as if holding its breath. She glanced down at her hand, flexing her fingers. The tingling was gone, but a subtle sense of disquiet remained.

She shook off the feeling, chiding herself for being overly sensitive. Accidents happened, and there was no harm done. Returning to her work, she tried to recapture her earlier focus, but her thoughts kept drifting to Maggie's suggestion.

Could quantum entanglement truly be influencing her patients? And if so, what did that mean for her research?

The questions swirled, like leaves caught in an eddy, the answers elusive. As the night wore on, Isabella immersed herself in the results, unaware of the threads wrapping themselves around her—the unseen connections drawing tighter.

When she finally left for the night, the corridors were deserted, the building silent. Stepping outside, she was greeted by the glittering array of constellations scattered across the sky. Though each one was distant they were all connected, a vast array of possibilities. Tomorrow, she hoped, would bring the clarity she needed. She dismissed the accident as just one of those things.

Accidents do happen, don't they?

10 – AN UNEXPECTED ENCOUNTER

"Fate deals the cards, but unseen hands have stacked the deck."

The Dolce Vita Café, 2A Kensington High Street, London W8 4PT - 12:05 PM, February 26

Isabella pushed open the door to the café, a haven where the aroma of freshly brewed coffee mingled with the soft murmur of conversation. The warmth inside welcoming, a gentle contrast to the unusually crisp chill of the afternoon. Her eyes scanned the room until they settled on Maggie, seated at a cosy corner table by the window. A smile of relief touched Isabella's lips—until she noticed the man sitting next to her.

Zach Mondori.

Her heart skipped a beat, a subtle heat rising within her. Of all people, why was Zach here? She felt a sudden flutter of nerves as approached, chiding herself for the unexpected reaction. It was just a friendly lunch... wasn't it?

"Isabella! Over here," Maggie called out, waving with a welcoming grin. "I hope you don't mind—I bumped into

Zach nearby and thought, why not?"

She mustered a smile, striving to steady the flutters she felt. "No, of course not. What a... pleasant surprise." Her eyes met Zach's, his usually composed expression warming in her presence.

"Hello again," he said. He sounded as smooth and engaging as she remembered. "I didn't expect to see you today."

"Nor did I," she replied, settling into the chair opposite him. Their gazes locked briefly before she glanced away, the atmosphere tinged with an unspoken awareness.

Maggie, ever the organiser, leaned back with an easy smile. "I'll just fetch us some drinks—cappuccino for you, Isabella? Zach, your usual?"

He chuckled softly. "You know me too well."

Isabella nodded, her pulse quickening as her workmate stood up. Turning her attention back to Zach, she found him relaxed, a touch of amusement dancing in his eyes.

"So, how is your project progressing?" she asked, hoping to steer the conversation onto neutral ground.

His eyes brightened, full of enthusiasm. "It's fascinating. We're making significant strides. Temporal stabilization remains challenging, but each experiment brings us closer."

She leaned in, genuinely intrigued. "Have you managed to minimise the variances you mentioned?"

He nodded, his hands animated as he explained. "We're experimenting with lower power levels to stabilise the bridge. The challenge is that reducing the energy input leaves too small a window of opportunity. It's a delicate balance between strength and stability. But I believe we're close to resolving it. We've moved to shift work, testing overnight and on weekends. The board wants the prototype presented to the press in a few weeks. We're on the brink." His excitement was palpable, rekindling a familiar passion within her.

As he spoke, she watched him, captivated by the intensity in his gaze. There was something magnetic about the way he conveyed his ideas, his entire being resonating with energy. She found herself drawn not only to his words but to the earnestness behind them.

Maggie returned with their drinks, placing them on the table with a smile. "Well, I hate to dash off, but I have a prior engagement," she announced, standing and gathering her bag. "You two enjoy the rest of the afternoon."

Isabella blinked, surprised by her sudden departure. "Oh, are you sure?"

Maggie gave a knowing smile. "Absolutely. You both seem to have plenty to discuss."

With a quick wave and a discreet wink in Isabella's direction, she slipped out the door, leaving them alone. Silence reigned, the air between them rich with possibilities.

"Well, hello again. What are the chances?" Zach jumped in quickly, his gaze meeting hers with a newfound softness.

She felt a blush rise in her cheeks, hastily taking a sip of her coffee to hide it.

"Yes, quite a surprise. But it's a pleasant one."

He smiled, his eyes holding hers a fraction longer than needed. "You know, I've been meaning to ask about your work. Maggie mentioned you're exploring temporal entanglement to combat neurodegenerative diseases?"

Isabella nodded, her initial shyness giving way to enthusiasm. "Yes, it's complex but promising. We're hoping to reverse the effects of conditions like Alzheimer's by essentially 'resetting' neural pathways."

"That's incredible," Zach said, genuine admiration in his tone. "There's more overlap between our fields than I realised. Quantum entanglement, temporal shifts— we're both attempting to bend the rules of time in our own ways."

She smiled, the tension easing. "It does seem that way. It's interesting how different projects can converge unexpectedly."

He leaned forward slightly, his expression thoughtful. "It's more than interesting. It feels... significant."

Her heart quickened at his words, the atmosphere between them growing more intimate. For countless moments, she allowed herself to imagine stepping beyond the confines of her current life, embracing something new, something more fulfilling.

But before she could delve further, a clatter from inside the café drew their attention. A staff member had dropped a tray, and the brief commotion broke the spell. Isabella glanced out the window and noticed a shadowy figure standing across the street, watching them.

Her brow furrowed. "Who is that...?"

Zach followed her gaze, his curiosity piqued.. "Someone you know?"

She dismissed his question, a subtle unease creeping in. "No... I don't think so."

The figure melted into the surroundings, leaving her with a lingering sense of disquiet. She pushed the thought aside, turning back to him with a reassuring smile. "Sorry about that. Where were we?"

He chuckled softly. "I believe we were discussing the mysteries of the universe—and how we might solve them together."

As their conversation flowed, she couldn't help but feel that something more profound than scientific discovery was going on. There was a connection here, unexpected yet undeniable. She felt a spark of genuine excitement bursting into flames.

Unbeknownst to them, across the street, a figure lingered briefly before disappearing into the throng of pedestrians. A message was sent.

Keane and Mondori alone together at café.

The text appeared on Davina Drake's phone. She glanced at it, a sly smile curving her lips.

"Very interesting indeed," she murmured to herself.

11 – A CRACK IN THE FOUNDATIONS

"When foundations falter, chaos rushes in to fill the void."

The Keane residence, Russell Square Mansions, 12 Russell Square, Bloomsbury, London, WC1B 5BG – 07:20 AM, February 27

Steam clung to the bathroom mirror as Isabella gripped the cool porcelain of the sink, her damp skin still tingling from the heat of the shower. She gazed into her reflection, searching her eyes for any signs of change. Outwardly, her face remained the same, but deep down, she knew something was different.

She rinsed her face, hoping to wash away the memories that weren't her own—the uninvited thoughts arriving without warning. They were becoming more frequent now, each one pulling her closer to a surrender she wasn't sure she could resist. And then there was Zach.

Temptation, it seemed, was gaining the upper hand.

Her phone vibrated on the counter, an unwelcome tether to reality. She didn't need to look to know it was James, back in the country, probably suggesting dinner. A mix of irritation and guilt washed over her. The prospect of sitting across from him, engaging in forced pleasantries, felt unbearable. She couldn't bring herself to respond. Slipping the phone into her pocket, she left the bathroom. Dealing with James could wait. For now, more pressing matters demanded her attention: breakfast, the school run, and the board report that could no longer be postponed. Duty called.

***

Running late once again, Isabella stepped out onto the bustling streets of Bloomsbury, already alive with the steady rhythm of commuters. Time marched forward, indifferent to her readiness. She approached Aldwych Station, its familiar old entrance tucked away like a forgotten relic of the city.

Descending the steps to her first transit point, she joined the flow of people—a constant stream of strangers heading toward their own obligations. The Piccadilly Line train arrived with a gust of air, and she slipped inside, taking the first available seat.

The train rattled onward, tunnel walls flashing past in alternating shadows and light. She gazed absently, barely registering the journey. It had become mere routine. At Holborn, she transferred to the Central Line without conscious thought, following her habitual path. Commuters ebbed and flowed around her, a sea of faces she seldom noticed.

Arriving at Bank, Isabella moved with the throng, switching to the DLR for the final leg. The atmosphere shifted palpably as Canary Wharf loomed ahead. Crystal towers rose like impassive sentinels, cold and unfeeling, as the train carried her into the financial heart of the city.

Emerging onto the bustling pavement, she stood before the majestic twin peaks of the Daystrom Institute. Its sleek lines soared skyward, reaching for the clouds as if the building itself sought to escape the worries of the world beneath.

Maggie was waiting for her, leaning against a desk, the usual enigmatic smile was tempered slightly. For some reason, she looked a little older with every passing day. Isabella wondered what her colleague had in store for her today.

"You look exhausted," Maggie observed softly, handing her a steaming cup of coffee. "Late night?"

Isabella nodded, accepting the drink gratefully. "I haven't been sleeping well. There's a lot on my mind. What about you? Still working all hours of the day and night?"

Maggie's gaze sharpened as she studied her closely, ignoring Isabella's observation. "You're under immense pressure," she said gently. "It's no wonder your *imagination* is playing tricks on you." She emphasised the word "imagination," almost challenging Isabella to dispute it.

Uncertain whether to find comfort or unease in her words, What wasn't she saying?

Setting down her bag, Isabella retrieved a folder from her drawer and leaned against the desk, opening the file. "I've been reviewing the data," she said quietly. "There's something... off. The errors—they seem almost intentional."

Maggie's eyes darkened slightly as she leaned in. "What are you saying?"

Isabella hesitated, but before she could elaborate, Ted appeared unexpectedly, his presence commanding immediate attention. His face was as inscrutable as ever, though a new crease on his brow hinted at underlying tension.

"Isabella, a word in my office. Now!"

Ted's tone left no room for negotiation. Maggie offered a sympathetic shrug as Isabella set down her coffee. Grabbing her notebook, she followed Ted out of the lab.

The late afternoon sun bled through the partially drawn blinds in Ted's office, casting stark shadows across the floor. He moved behind his desk but remained standing, his back to her as he gazed out over the skyline. The atmosphere was taut.

Closing the door behind her, Isabella waited, the silence stretching uncomfortably. She finally cleared her throat.

"You wanted to see me?"

Without turning, Ted spoke slowly, measuring his words. "Your project. The data. It doesn't add up."

She had anticipated this conversation, dreaded it even. Hearing the words made her stomach tighten. Swallowing the retort that sprang to mind, she forced herself to remain composed.

"I've noticed the anomalies as well," she reiterated. "I'm investigating possible causes."

He turned then, his expression unreadable. "It's more than mere anomalies, Isabella. There's something you're missing."

A spark of irritation flashed within her. Of course, there was something she hadn't identified—that's why they were anomalies. "What exactly do you think I'm overlooking?" she asked, keeping her tone measured.

He hesitated, choosing his words carefully. "What if the inconsistencies don't stem from experimental errors, but from some form of external interference?"

She frowned. "External interference? If you mean contamination, we've accounted for that."

"Not contamination," he corrected sharply. "Variables beyond standard control parameters. Phenomena unaccounted for in conventional models."

She studied him, trying to read between the lines. Ted was typically the embodiment of rationality, grounded in empirical evidence. Yet now, he spoke with a vagueness she'd not heard before.

"Ted, if you have something to say, please just say it."

He sighed, his shoulders dropping visibly. "I was hoping it wouldn't come to this, but perhaps it's time you're brought into the loop."

"What loop? What aren't you telling me?" she asked, caught off guard.

He stepped closer, lowering his voice as if wary of eavesdroppers. "The anomalies in your data align with events we've been monitoring—occurrences that defy our current understanding of quantum mechanics."

She blinked, struggling to process his words. "But that's impossible. Quantum effects haven't been observed in people."

"Until now," Ted replied. "Which is why this is critical.

We need to determine the cause."

A mix of personal frustration and professional curiosity welled up inside her. "What do you mean, until now? And what do you expect me to do?"

"We're bringing in additional resources," he said. "An expert from our quantum research division will join your team."

She stiffened. "You're replacing me?"

"No," he assured quickly. "But you'll need support—specialists in this area."

"When? Who?" she demanded.

"You've already met her on more than one occasion, I believe. Maggie Carter. She'll start officially with you tomorrow."

"Isabella?" Ted prompted, noticing her sudden silence. "Is there an issue?"

She blinked, refocusing. "Sorry, it's just... Maggie Carter?"

"Yes. Why do you ask?"

"I'm... not sure," she managed, her voice trailing off. Was she being paranoid? The woman clearly knew her subject. Perhaps it made sense for her to assist. Didn't it?

Ted considered her words before nodding. "No further debate then; the decision is final."

She steadied herself. "Okay. If there's more I need to know, I'd appreciate complete transparency."

His gaze softened slightly. "I understand this is a lot to take in. We'll discuss the details later. For now, try to get some rest."

Isabella nodded numbly and turned to leave. As she reached the door, Ted's voice stopped her.

"And Isabella?"

She glanced back.

"Be careful," he said quietly. "We're treading on delicate ground."

She gave the softest of smiles. "Aren't we always?"

Leaving his office, her apprehension grew further. Too many coincidences were piling up. Questions swirled in her mind, but one stood out. *What was really going on?*

***

Returning to the lab, she found Maggie engrossed in a data sheet, her demeanour calm and unreadable. Isabella approached cautiously. "I hear we'll be working together more closely," she said, attempting to sound casual.

Maggie looked up, a cheeky smile playing at the corners of her mouth. "Yes, Ted mentioned it. I'm looking forward to it."

"Funny, he only just told me," Isabella remarked, searching Maggie's eyes for any sign of ulterior motives.

"Communication can be a bit fragmented around here," Maggie replied smoothly. "But I'm glad. I think we make a good team."

Isabella forced a smile. "I suppose we do."

As the afternoon wore on, they worked side by side, yet an invisible barrier seemed to separate them. Isabella could feel that beneath her friendly exterior lay hidden intentions.

When the clock edged toward evening, Isabella began gathering her things. "I think I'll call it a day," she said lightly.

"Good idea," Maggie agreed. "Rest is important."

As Isabella left the lab, she glanced back to see Maggie watching her, an inscrutable expression on her face.

***

Aldwych Tube Station The Strand, London, WC2R 1EP –

07:00 PM, February 27

That evening, the journey home felt interminable. Isabella longed for the sanctuary of her apartment, a brief respite from the turmoil swirling in her mind. Yet less than two blocks from home, her sixth sense kicked in. She glanced around the dimly lit street, shadows stretching beneath flickering lampposts. Nothing appeared amiss, yet the feeling of being watched persisted.

Exiting Aldwych Station, she took the quickest route back as the streets emptied, late stragglers making their way home. Turning the final corner, she spotted James standing outside their building. His coat was pulled tight against the evening chill, shoulders tense as if bracing against more than the cold. He hadn't noticed her approach, his gaze set on the pavement. Her heart sank; she recognised this stance—it meant he was troubled.

As she neared, he looked up, eyes clouded with worry and frustration. The tension tightened between them with each step.

"Isabella," he called out, straining. "We need to talk."

She folded her arms around herself, a subconscious barrier. "About what?"

He hesitated, glancing toward the entrance before

meeting her gaze. "About us. About... everything."

She couldn't do this. Not now. She wasn't ready—perhaps she never would be. "Can't it wait?" she murmured. "It's been a long day."

"No, it can't." James replied firmly. "Something's changed. You've been distant. Different. I just want to understand."

She sighed, the persistence of his questioning pressing upon her. "I'm just tired, James. Work has been overwhelming."

He studied her face, searching for answers. "We both have demanding jobs, and I know I'm not perfect, but this feels like more than just stress. You're here, but it's as if you're somewhere else entirely."

They entered the building, the soft hum of hallway lights filling the silence. Climbing the stairs, she kept her gaze ahead, counting each step as a distraction.

"Talk to me," he urged. "Please."

She swallowed hard. How could she explain the inexplicable—the threads of another life weaving into her own? "There's nothing to discuss," she whispered.

Inside the apartment, she set her bag on the counter, her back still turned to him. The familiar surroundings offered no comfort tonight.

"Isabella," James pressed. "We're drifting apart. I don't know what's happening or why, but I don't want to lose you."

She turned toward him, meeting his desperate gaze. The concern etched on his face tugged at her defences. "I just need some space," she said softly.

"Space?" he echoed, hurt flickering across his face. "From me?"

"From everything," she replied, her eyes pleading for understanding.

He ran both hands through his hair, frustration evident. "I can't help if you shut me out. We're supposed to face things together."

"I know," she whispered. "It's just... complicated."

"Then simplify it," he responded tightly. "Don't block me out."

A surge of emotion welled within her—guilt, fear, an unnamed longing. "I wish I could," she admitted. "But I don't even understand it myself."

He took a step closer. "Is there someone else?"

The question hit home, sharp and unexpected. Her eyes

widened. "What? No! How could you think that?"

"Because I don't know what else to believe!" he exclaimed. "You're miles away even when you're right here. If there's something you're hiding, I need to know."

"There's no one else," she insisted, her voice trembling. "Please, believe me."

He searched her face, his expression softening slightly. "Then what is it? Whatever it is, we can face it together."

She looked away, blinking back tears. "I can't explain. It's just..."

Silence ensued. James sighed deeply, the fight draining out of him. "I hate seeing us like this," he said quietly.

"I'm sorry," she replied, her heart aching.

He reached out as if to touch her arm but hesitated. "Just... promise me you'll talk to someone. If not me, then perhaps a professional."

She nodded faintly, words failing her, and the chasm between them felt wider than ever.

"I'm going to bed," he said after a moment. "We can finish this tomorrow."

He paused, then leaned in to kiss her forehead—a gesture both familiar and distant. She pulled back instinctively.

"Goodnight," she murmured, watching as he walked down the hallway and disappeared into the guest room.

Alone in the dim light of the kitchen, Isabella sank into a chair. The quiet tick of the clock was the only sound in the otherwise oppressive silence. She buried her face in her hands.

Eventually, exhaustion propelled her to her feet. She headed to bed, checking that James had indeed taken the spare room. He lay facing away, his breathing steady yet shallow. Retreating to the master bedroom, she stared at the ceiling, sleep eluding her as fragmented images swirled in her mind—Zach's intense gaze, his words, echoes and elusive whispers.

Sometime deep in the night, she drifted into a restless slumber, the boundaries between dreams and reality blurring as threads of another existence wove themselves into her subconscious.

Firm hands shook her, pulling her abruptly from sleep. "Isabella," James's voice cut through the haze.

She blinked awake, disoriented. "What is it?"

He loomed over her, anger flooding his face. "Who is Zach?"

The colour drained from her cheeks, eyes wide with shock. "What?"

"I heard you last night, in bed." he said, eyes searching hers. "You kept repeating his name; 'Zach'. Are you involved with him?"

She stared at him, mind racing. "I... of course not. Don't be absurd."

"Don't lie to me," he snapped, hurt flashing in his eyes. "Is he why you've been so distant?"

"James, I swear, Zach is just a colleague," she pleaded. "That's all. I can't even remember what I was dreaming."

"A colleague?" he repeated sceptically. "You were calling out to him like you knew him intimately."

She sat up, desperation clear in her voice. "That's not true. Please, you have to trust me."

His eyes narrowed, jealousy seeping into his tone. "It's all starting to make sense. I suspected something was off." His fist slammed onto the bedside table, causing objects to scatter.

She recoiled, fear gripping her. "James, please..."

He turned slightly away, closing down the conversation. "This isn't over. Not by a long shot."

He stormed out, the door closing sharply behind him.

Left in the dim light, Isabella felt the silence envelop her. Sleep was impossible now. Her thoughts lingered on the man who had stirred such turmoil. Zach. Her heart was caught between temptation and guilt, her mind tethered to visions that defied explanation. She felt trapped between two worlds, neither offering solace. And one question echoed louder than all others.

"Where was this all leading to?"

12 – TWO HALVES MAKE A WHOLE

"In preparing for battle, I have always found that plans are useless, but planning is indispensable."

The Daystrom Institute, Level 75, Meridian Tower, 12 Meridian Place, Canary Wharf, London – 6:50 PM, March 1

The following days blurred into a haze of repetitive testing and a growing disconnect from the people and things that once mattered most to Isabella. She moved through the motions at work and home, but her mind was adrift, floating on an ocean of emotions—present in body but elsewhere in spirit.

As Ted had promised, Maggie and other specialists from the Quantum Research Division filtered through her lab, scrutinizing her findings and gathering in hushed clusters to discuss theories. Each new face sparked a fleeting surge of anticipation, swiftly followed by the inevitable disappointment of not seeing the one man she yearned to meet.

Returning to her workspace, the sterile familiarity of the lab enveloped her. The building was quieter than usual—most staff had left for the evening—but Maggie remained at her station, waiting like clockwork. The faint smile she offered seemed unconvincing. She was always there—watchful—her presence now more of a shadow, lingering at the periphery of Isabella's life. What once felt comforting had become... intrusive.

"Working late again?" her colleague inquired, her face illuminated by a small, welcoming smile.

Isabella stepped inside, her expression neutral yet observant. "Looks like I'm not the only one," she replied, setting her bag down. "You must be pulling double shifts."

Maggie waved off the remark. "Consultancy life—overtime comes with the territory. But what about you? How are things... really?"

Isabella paused, caught off guard by the personal question. "It's been... one of those days," she answered evasively.

Maggie tilted her head, curiosity clear. "What's that supposed to mean?"

She hesitated. Maggie had a knack for asking questions—subtle at first, then pressing just enough to make Isabella feel cornered. Her timing was impeccable, nudging Isabella when her defences were weakest. Coincidence? It was too consistent to ignore.

"Things just feel... strange," Isabella continued, shaking her head as if to clear a fog. "I can't quite explain it."

Maggie's eyes sharpened, locking onto hers. "Stop brushing it off, Bella. You know something is happening, and it's time to face it." There was a sudden force in her voice that startled Isabella, cutting through her thoughts like a blade.

She was taken by the intensity of those words. No one had ever spoken to her with such certainty, and it unsettled her deeply. Moreover, Maggie had called her "Bella," not "Isabella." Only her father had ever used that name. How could she possibly know that?

"What are you talking about?" Isabella's voice rose, confusion creasing her brow. "How do you know so much about me? What are you implying?

Maggie stepped closer, her demeanour serious—gone was the easy-going consultant. "I've been keeping an eye on you, watching. You're not imagining things, and you're definitely not losing your mind. What you're experiencing is connected to your research with Zach. And it's far more complex than you realise."

Isabella felt dizzy. Maggie's words struck home like a physical blow. She had harboured suspicions, yes, but hearing them confirmed left her reeling. The trust she'd placed in this woman now felt precarious, perhaps even dangerous.

"How... how do you know about my situation?" Isabella stammered, her voice trembling. She hadn't confided in anyone—not even Ted—about the intimate, almost feverish dreams she'd been having about Zach.

Unflinching, Maggie's gaze remained steady. "The dreams about him? About Zach? I know because I've had them too."

Isabella froze. Her heart pounded violently, breath catching in her throat. Zach—the man who filled her secret dreams with fierce, undeniable longing. She hadn't told a soul.

"What?" Her voice was a mere whisper, her mind spinning. "I've never mentioned him to anyone."

"They're not dreams, Isabella," Maggie interrupted softly but firmly, each word slicing through her disbelief. "They're not figments of your imagination either."

Isabella's mind was in turmoil. How could she know her most intimate thoughts and deepest desires?

Her voice wavered. "This... this doesn't make sense. Who are you? *What* are you?"

Maggie moved closer, gently placing a hand on her arm, her expression more understanding than ever. "I know it's hard to process. But trust me, you're not alone in this. Whatever's happening—we're in it together. We need to fix this, to prevent it from happening again," urgency in her tone.

Isabella stared at her, caught in a whirlwind of confusion, fear, and incredulity. The words echoed in her mind, and despite the absurdity of it all, one thing was clear—Maggie knew too much. She wasn't lying.

She nodded shakily. "Where do we start?"

Maggie reached for a stack of files, pulling them closer. "Let's begin with what we have. We need to identify the trigger."

Together, they delved into the data, cross-referencing files and running simulations. Determination overshadowed the fatigue setting in. Piece by piece, they assembled the puzzle, weaving together knowns and unknowns. The room darkened as hours passed, but they pressed on into the night. They worked seamlessly, like two halves of a whole.

***

The Daystrom Institute, Level 75, Meridian Tower, 12 Meridian Place, Canary Wharf, London – 9:40 AM, March 2

The following day, Isabella found herself pacing outside

Ted's office. Maggie had been right—he was still withholding information, and it was time to confront him. The door was slightly ajar, and as she approached, hushed voices reached her ears. She hesitated, hand hovering over the handle, straining to catch snippets of the conversation.

"You don't understand, Davina," Ted's voice was low and tense. "This isn't just about the research anymore. We've opened Pandora's box. It's escalating. If we don't contain it, we could all lose everything."

Isabella's breath caught. Davina Drake? What was she doing here?

Davina's voice, smooth and cold, slipped through the crack. "You've been cautious, Ted. But caution is a luxury we can no longer afford. We need answers—I need answers."

"We can't rush this," Ted replied tightly. "We're dealing with forces beyond our comprehension. If we push too hard, the consequences could be catastrophic."

"Catastrophic?" Davina's tone sharpened. "Or profitable? Don't delude yourself. Those funding this project are indifferent to risks. They crave control."

Shock rippled through Isabella. This wasn't just about the research—something far darker was at play, and Davina was pulling the strings.

Before she could fully process what was being said, the door swung open. Ted stood in the doorway, his face pale, eyes widening in surprise.

"Isabella, what are you doing here? What did you hear?"

She swallowed hard, striving to steady her voice. "Ted, we need to talk. About the project."

His expression darkened. "Now isn't the time."

"It is the time," she insisted, her voice resolute. "I know you're hiding something. I heard you just now. I want the truth."

Ted stepped out, closing the door firmly behind him. Taking her arm gently, he guided her down the corridor toward the breakout area.

"This isn't a conversation for here," he murmured. "Not now."

"Why not?" Isabella retorted, narrowing her eyes. "What are you so afraid of?"

"I'm trying to protect you," he muttered. "There are things—I should have told you."

Her heart raced. "What things?"

He glanced around nervously before meeting her gaze,

guilt etched on his features. "What's happening to your patients isn't random. It's linked to the Quantum Bridge experiments."

Her eyes widened in shock. The issues with her research were connected to Zach's work. He had known all along.

"But what does that have to do with me?" she asked, her voice shaking. "Why is it affecting me too?"

Ted hesitated, his eyes flickering toward the closed door. "Why it's impacting you directly, I can't explain. I genuinely don't know."

He paused, the silence deafening.

"But there's more," he continued quietly. "This isn't just about you or your patients, Isabella."

"What do you mean, there's more?", she asked.

His answer was ominous.

"I think time may be slipping away for all of us."

13 – DREAMS OF FUTURES PAST

"The future is always a projection of the present and our choices therein."

The Keane residence, Russell Square Mansions, 12 Russell Square, Bloomsbury, London, WC1B 5BG – 06:55 AM, March 5

Morning light filtered through Isabella's curtains, casting soft, shifting shadows across the floor. She lay motionless, eyes fixed on the ceiling, her thoughts entangled in a chaotic web. Sleep had evaded her, haunted by vivid flashes of memories that weren't hers, playing out like a film she couldn't pause.

Each time she closed her eyes, she was somewhere else—lost in a world with him.

With a sigh, she pushed the blankets aside and sat up. James was back in Brussels; they hadn't revisited their argument, and she couldn't afford distractions now. The project demanded her full attention, yet the conversations with Maggie and Ted nagged at her—something they'd said hovered just out of reach, like a forgotten dream.

Moving mechanically through the morning, she prepared breakfast for herself and Katie. But everything about her home felt off, despite its pristine appearance. The kitchen was immaculate, counters gleaming to the point of sterility. Why was she always polishing, always tidying? She wondered if leaving a little mess might make life feel less constrained—less boxed in.

Her gaze drifted to the grandfather clock in the corner, its pendulum swings louder than usual, each tick pounding in her head. Time marched on relentlessly, dragging her along whether she was ready or not. The clock didn't care; its hands kept turning, round and round, like the loop her life had become—predictable, never-ending.

Yet, something inside her was changing. New desires pushed aside old ways of thinking, opening her mind to possibilities she'd never dared consider. Why did she feel the urge to leave the house in disarray, to step outside in her pyjamas and dance in the street? She no longer wanted the life she'd carefully curated. She needed to break free, to explore. She needed to see *him*.

***

The Daystrom Institute, Level 75, Meridian Tower, 12 Meridian Place, Canary Wharf, London – 2:22 PM, March 5

The day unfolded in a blur of activity, though Isabella struggled to focus on her tasks. Her "episodes," as she'd begun to call them, grew more vivid as time passed. What were once fleeting impressions had become intensely real. She could see more clearly, feel sensations as if she were truly there—the perfume of flowers, the warmth of an open fire. Increasingly, she questioned which life was real and which was merely a dream.

Meanwhile, the data that had once mocked Isabella with its inconsistencies was finally beginning to reveal a pattern. Maggie remained constantly by her side, a steadfast presence offering support and insights. Together, they formed a formidable team, and by late afternoon, they were steps closer to understanding what was happening.

"Look at this," Maggie said, pointing to a sequence on the screen. "These fluctuations correspond precisely with the temporal anomalies you've been experiencing."

Isabella leaned in, her eyes scanning the data. "You're right. It's almost as if..."

Her words trailed off as her the world around her began to spin. The room seemed to tilt, and the fluorescent lights flickered erratically.

"Did you feel that?" Isabella asked, leaning against the desk to steady herself.

Maggie turned to her, concern etched on her face. "Feel what?"

In that very moment, whilst Isabella tried to process the question, Maggie's form suddenly began to shimmer, her outline blurring as if she were a reflection on disturbed water.

"Maggie!" Isabella exclaimed, reaching out instinctively.

Maggie looked down at her own hands, eyes widening in panic as they faded in and out of focus. "Isabella, what's happening?" her voice wavered, nothing more than a twisted echo.

Isabella's heart pounded. The lab around them distorted, walls stretching and contracting as if viewed through a fisheye lens. Sounds became muffled, replaced by a low-pitched pulse that drowned out all else.

"Maggie, hold on!" Isabella shouted, though her voice sounded distant even to herself.

Maggie's body flickered, momentarily disappearing before reappearing a few seconds later. She reached out toward Isabella, but her hand passed through the desk as though it were insubstantial.

"I can't... I can't control it!" Maggie's voice was laced with fear.

Isabella felt her panic rising. "This isn't real. It can't be," she whispered, squeezing her eyes shut in a desperate attempt to steady herself.

When she opened them, the disorientation intensified. Colours bled into one another, and the equipment warped into unrecognizable shapes. Isabella's vision blurred, and she felt herself swaying, the ground beneath her shifting like waves beneath a boat.

Suddenly, a sharp snap rang in her ears, and everything stilled. The lab was quiet. The lights were steady. The sounds of humming equipment returned to normal.

Isabella stood alone, her hand still outstretched to where Maggie had been moments before. She spun around, searching the room. "Maggie?" she called out, her voice echoing in the empty space.

There was no response. The lab was silent, everyone had left for the day. Glancing at the clock on the wall, Isabella's stomach dropped—hours had passed in what felt like mere moments. Her mind raced. Had she imagined the entire episode?

She took a breath, trying to calm herself. There was no one to make excuses to; the lab was deserted.

Isabella grabbed her bag. She couldn't stay there any longer. Enough was enough. She left the lab and boarded the first train from Canary Wharf, heading straight into the heart of London.

***

Kensington Gardens, London W8 4PT - 7:40 PM, March 5

By the time she arrived, the sun was setting, painting the skyline in vibrant hues of orange and gold. Her destination was Kensington Gardens, the memory of her earlier encounter replaying endlessly in her mind. She had to see him again. She simply had to.

The park was quieter than usual, the evening air cool against her skin as she wandered along the tree-lined paths. Her footsteps crunched softly on the gravel, and for just an instant, it felt as if she were the only person in the world. A sudden breeze brushed her face, a light-headedness enveloping her, as though predicting what was about to happen.

And then she saw *him*.

He stood near the water's edge, his back turned, hands casually tucked into his pockets. The sight of him sent a rush of excitement coursing through her—a pull she couldn't ignore. She hesitated, remnants of her old self whispering caution, urging her to stop. But the fire igniting within her, a deep yearning, overpowered those faint protests. She moved forward.

As she approached, he turned, their eyes locking with the same intensity she'd felt before. It was as if he'd been waiting for her all along, knowing she would come.

"You," he said, his words stirring her emotions. "I've been waiting."

Isabella's heart raced. None of this made logical sense—the inexplicable pull toward a man she'd only recently met. Yet it was undeniable, an irresistible force defying explanation.

She took a hesitant step closer, her gaze searching his face. "Why do I feel like I know you so well? Why do I want you, need you?" The words spilled out, her restraint dissolving in the heat of these strange new emotions.

He looked equally perplexed, though a glimmer of understanding shone in his eyes. "I've been asking myself the same," he admitted, betraying his emotions.

"Are you certain we've never crossed paths before, in a previous life?" she suggested, though even as she spoke, she knew it wasn't true.

His smile said it all. "If we had, I wouldn't have forgotten."

A comfortable silence settled between them, filled with unspoken emotion. Slowly, he extended his hand, waiting for her to take it.

The moment their fingers intertwined, a surge of electricity seemed to pass between them. She gasped but didn't pull away, unwilling to break the connection.

Their eyes remained locked, fascination deepening. He took her other hand, drawing her closer, the quiet evening serving as the perfect backdrop. She didn't resist, surrendering her senses to the subtle scent of his cologne.

He was so close now, their faces mere inches apart. A rush of heat flooded through her.

And waited.

Time seemed to blur. Each moment drew her deeper into the intensity of their connection. Her thoughts aligned, the last remnants of caution slipping away as emotion consumed her, guiding her into uncharted territory. It felt as though the world shifted beneath her, as if she were stepping out of one life and into another—a new existence where they were all that mattered.

***

Zach's Apartment, Meridian Court, 32 Greenwich High Road, London SE10 8JL – 06:22 AM, March 6

Isabella stirred, the heat of the night lingering on her body. Soft morning light filtered through the curtains, bathing the room in strands of glittering ruby and gold. She blinked, her mind catching up with her surroundings. She wasn't at home.

She was in Zach's apartment.

Her gaze wandered—the rich, dark wood of the furniture, the opulent Victorian décor, large leather sofas adorned with plush cushions. It felt worlds apart from her own space, a place imbued with intensity and passion, mirroring the night they'd shared. It was eerily familiar. She'd seen this room before, but where?

Her heart swelled, an overwhelming flood of emotions threatening to consume her anew. She could still feel the heat of his body against hers, the raw magnetism that had drawn them together, as if every nerve in her body resonated with him. The memory of his touch sent a shiver through her—gentle yet insistent, each caress a silent invitation for more. Their bodies had merged effortlessly, as though destined to find one another in this way. She could taste the lingering essence of his kiss, the intoxicating blend of closeness and desire clinging to her senses, leaving her yearning even now.

Each embrace had been a deliberate surrender. His lips explored hers with a fervour that seemed boundless, igniting a flame within that burned ever brighter. His presence was all she needed in that place where time ceased to make sense. Each word they whispered, each breath the shared, carried an intensity beyond mere attraction, as if they had crossed an unseen threshold together, drawn together by forces beyond their comprehension.

She had given herself to him completely, waves of emotion sweeping her along, leaving no room for any doubt or hesitation. With every sigh, every lingering touch she fell deeper, until their boundaries blurred. They became one and the same. The night seemed to last forever, imbued with an energy that left them both trembling, their hearts pounding long after they'd lain entwined, spent and yet still insatiable in their desire.

Turning her head, Zach lay beside her, his breath rising and falling in the cyclic rhythm of sleep. The hazing light of dawn accentuated the contours of his face, his features softened in repose. Something more than mere attraction gripped her—a tenderness toward him that filled her with both joy and vulnerability.

For many moments, she lay silently watching him, absorbing the serenity of the scene. She had lost herself in his arms, and now, in the early light of day, she knew she would never be the same again.

***

Zach's Apartment, Meridian Court, 32 Greenwich High Road, London SE10 8JL – 07:05 AM, March 6

Breakfast felt unusually delightful, the silence golden

between them. She hesitated before speaking, searching for a way to broach the subject.

"This might sound strange," she began softly, "but... have you been experiencing anything unusual lately?"

Zach paused, fork hovering mid-air, as if weighing how much to reveal. "Unusual in what way?"

"Dreams," she said carefully. "Or visions of places you've never been, people you've never met."

A flicker of recognition crossed his face. "Yes," he admitted. "I've had them. Glimpses of other lives—brief, but they feel real."

Relief washed over her. "I thought I was losing my mind."

"You're not," he reassured her. "I've wondered if it's tied to the project I'm working on. I thought perhaps you'd already figured that out."

Her heart quickened. She leaned in. "Do you think it could be connected to both of our projects?"

"It's possible," Zach mused. "If consciousness operates on a quantum level, your experiments might be affecting test subjects' perceptions. But I don't understand why it would impact you." He looked at her intently. "You haven't been experimenting on yourself, have you?"

His question unlocked the memory that had eluded her

—the spill. She'd accidentally gotten the compound on her hand. That's when it all began: the episodes, the vivid visions. The compound had heightened her mind's sensitivity, making her more receptive to the quantum shifts caused by Zach's experiments. Before the incident, she'd only been questioning her life choices. Now, her mind was opening to infinite possibilities.

Zach watched her, as if piecing together her thoughts. "Quantum entanglement," he said calmly but intensely. "When particles become linked, the state of one affects the other, no matter the distance. If our consciousnesses are somehow entangled..."

"Then our experiences might be overlapping," Isabella completed his sentence, eyes widening. "But that means we're interacting on a level beyond the physical."

"Exactly," he affirmed. "It might also explain the anomalies in my experiments. If human consciousness can influence quantum states, it could be causing the disturbances we're observing."

A shiver ran down her spine as the gravity of their situation sank in. "This is incredible—and unsettling."

He nodded solemnly. "Agreed. I have no idea where this could lead."

Reaching for a notebook filled with equations and notes, Zach continued, "I've been tracking these fluctuations for weeks. Initially, they were minor anomalies, statistical outliers. But they're occurring more frequently and growing stronger."

She leaned over, recognizing patterns in his data. "These fluctuations match the irregularities I've seen in neural activity during my tests."

His gaze sharpened. "You're certain?"

She nodded. "Patients reported vivid dreams, memories misaligned with their lives."

"You mean this version of their lives? Just like you?" he exclaimed.

"Yes," she continued, meeting his eyes. "Our work is causing this."

"It's possible," Zach said cautiously. "Or perhaps we're tapping into something already occurring."

"Like what?" she whispered.

He chose his words carefully. "If multiple realities exist and the boundaries between them are breaking down, they could start to overlap. People might begin to observe alternate versions of their lives, influenced by different choices they've made."

Isabella shuddered. "And our experiments are amplifying this effect?"

"Potentially," he agreed. "Your neural stimulation could heighten patients' abilities to perceive these overlaps, while my work might be destabilizing the boundaries that separate alternate realities."

She leaned back, mind reeling. "This is... beyond anything I imagined."

"Me too," Zach said gently. "But it could also be a breakthrough—an unprecedented opportunity to understand consciousness and reality."

"Or" she countered, her voice firm, "it could be dangerous. We might be endangering people—endangering ourselves."

His expression darkened. "That's what concerns me."

They sat in silence, the enormity of their discovery pressing upon them.

"What should we do?" Isabella asked finally, her voice steadying.

"We need to run joint experiments," Zach suggested. "We can see if our work connects. But we have to be careful." His tone was serious. "If anyone finds out what we're doing, they'll stop at nothing to take if from us."

She swallowed hard, the gravity of the situation becoming starkly clear. "This is worse than I imagined."

He reached out, his hand taking hers. "We're in this together. We'll find a way."

The gentleness of his touch moved her. "Thank you," she whispered. "I don't feel alone anymore."

A sweet, adorable smile appeared on his lips as he replied.

"Neither do I."

14 – A FORK IN THE ROAD

*"In a world of ever-changing questions,
our choices define our path."*

**Aldwych Tube Station The Strand, London, WC2R 1EP –
08:40 AM, March 6**

Isabella stepped out of Zach's apartment, the cool morning air brushing against her skin—so different to the lingering warmth of his touch. The world outside felt distant, muted, as if she were drifting through a dream. She descended the steps slowly, her legs still unsteady from the night before, her mind replaying the hours spent in his embrace. Each step felt lighter than the last, the vibrant hum of Greenwich unfolding around her—a bustling world somehow disconnected from the one she had just left.

The streets pulsed with life—buses rumbling past, people hurrying about their morning routines—but it all blurred into the background. She didn't notice the market stalls being set up or the cyclists weaving through traffic. Her thoughts were miles away, entangled in the memory of Zach's smile, the touch of his fingers, the way he had made her feel utterly alive. Moving through the crowd as if in a trance, her ten-minute walk to the overground station passed unnoticed, dulled by the intoxicating recollections of the night.

Reaching Aldwych Tube Station, she paused, blinking in surprise. She had arrived in what felt like the blink of an eye. Her feet had carried her on autopilot, her mind too clouded with thoughts of him to register her surroundings.

She tried to reset. *How did I get here?* she asked herself, though the answer was clear. She was still glowing, still enveloped in the afterglow of their time together. The night had consumed her so completely that everything else seemed insignificant compared to the memories she had made.

Taking a deep breath, she waited for the train, the burden of the challenges ahead beginning to pull her back to reality.

***

Daystrom Institute, Meridian Tower, 12 Meridian Place, Canary Wharf, London – *08:55 AM, March 6*

Standing in the shadow of the towering Daystrom building, Isabella felt surprisingly refreshed despite having been awake most of the night. A familiar arm looped through hers without warning.

"Morning. My, your cheeks are glowing. What have you

been up to? Are you ready?" Maggie's voice was almost playful, as though they were about to embark on an adventure together.

Isabella turned to her new friend, a flush of embarrassment warming her face. "Ready?"

"To take control of our little... situation," Maggie replied, her eyes locking onto Isabella's with intensity. "Time waits for no one. We can't sit around waiting for things to fall apart again. It's time to get our act together!"

"Any idea how we achieve that?" Isabella questioned, her tone puzzled but unusually upbeat. She even managed a wink and a smile, still buoyed by the lingering euphoria.

Maggie stepped closer, her expression softening as she placed a hand on Isabella's shoulder. "Perhaps you don't need to understand everything right now. You just have to trust yourself—your instincts. We know these episodes are connected to you and him, so maybe you two need to work on this problem together?"

Isabella smiled appreciatively. The woman seemed almost clairvoyant at times.

Continuing with a calm yet firm tone, Maggie said, "Ted's been keeping secrets, hiding the truth about the experiment. But we already suspected that. The problems started when the initial trials went awry, overloading the system. But what's happening to you now... it's different. There's something else at play."

"There is," Isabella responded immediately. "I spoke with Zach..." She hesitated before adding, "this morning. We might know what's causing these changes in me."

Maggie's eyes flickered with something—hesitation, perhaps—but she maintained her gaze. "Go on."

Isabella explained how her vivid dreams had begun after the incident with the chemical spill weeks earlier. Maggie listened intently, nodding as Isabella shared her conversation with Zach.

"That explains it," came the prompt response, her voice quickening as she connected the dots. "That's the missing variable. I knew it! It never happened in my..." She stopped abruptly, realizing she risked revealing too much.

"Go on. What were you about to say?" Isabella pressed, her tone insistent.

Attempting to deflect, Maggie replied, "I told you I was part of the experiment."

Isabella nodded slowly, not convinced by her response.

Maggie's expression turned serious. "I was. But not in the way you think. The work we were doing wasn't just an exploration of parallel realities—it was an attempt to manipulate history."

The words hung heavily between them, laden with implication. Isabella felt the ground shift beneath her, her world tilting once more. So that was the crux of it—controlling time, altering reality.

"Why didn't you tell me this before?" Isabella asked, a sense of her duplicity creeping in. "Why keep this from me?"

Maggie sighed, her hand dropping from Isabella's shoulder. "I wanted to protect you. Involving you meant exposing you to powerful forces. But now... there's no choice. The disturbances are escalating faster than ever, and you're the key—the unknown variable causing it."

Isabella struggled to process what she'd just heard. The key? How could she be central to stopping something she scarcely understood?

Before she could voice her questions, Maggie continued, her tone urgent. "These fractures in time and space have become linked to your emotional state. The compound you came into contact with acts as an accelerant, intensifying them for you. The more conflicted you are emotionally, the more intense they become. Every doubt, every choice you make, every feeling you have—it affects the balance of other realities. Right now, that balance is collapsing."

A wave of unease washed over Isabella. If the disruptions were tied to her emotions, to her decisions, it made a twisted kind of sense. Each time she thought of Zach, each time she felt that inexorable pull towards him, the episodes grew more frequent, more intense. Her emotional turmoil was fuelling the fractures.

"But how do I stop it?" she asked, her confidence waning. "I don't know how to control any of this."

Maggie's expression softened, her eyes filled with empathy. "It's not about control; it's about acceptance. You can't fight this—you have to embrace it. Accept that there are different versions of you, different lives you could lead. Then, you have to choose."

"Choose?" Isabella echoed, her eyes narrowing. "Choose what?"

Maggie hesitated, her gaze momentarily drifting before meeting Isabella's again. "You have to decide which life you want to live. Right now, you're caught between possibilities—between the life you have and the one you've glimpsed. The disturbances reflect the tension of that conflict. Until you make a choice, they'll continue to grow, widening the fractures between realities."

She held her breath, the magnitude of the words sinking in. The anomalies weren't random—they were intrinsically linked to her emotional state. Her indecision, her inability to choose between the known and the desired, was destabilizing reality itself.

"How do you know all this?" Isabella asked, suspicion creeping in. "How can you be so certain?"

Maggie's eyes darkened, and for the first time, Isabella glimpsed a shadow behind her friend's usual warmth. "Because I've slipped through the cracks myself. I made the wrong choice long ago, and I've been living with the consequences ever since."

A cold chill ran down her spine. What choice had Maggie made? What consequences had she endured?

Before she could ask, Maggie stepped closer, keeping her voice down. "I told you. You're not the first to experience this. It's happened before. But this time, the stakes are much higher. This time we risk breaking everything."

***

Daystrom Institute, Meridian Tower, 12 Meridian Place, Canary Wharf, London – *2:15 PM, March 6*

After a working lunch with colleagues discussing their latest findings, Isabella returned to the office. The conversation had been engaging, but her mind kept drifting back to the events of the past twenty-four hours. As she stepped into the lift, she realised she wasn't alone.

Zach stood near the back, alongside a few others returning to their desks. He glanced up, catching her eye briefly, and offered a trademark smile that sent a pleasant shiver down her spine. She returned his smile, her eyes reflecting the passion they had shared.

She moved towards the rear, positioning herself beside him, the space between them charged with unspoken tension. Their hands hung at their sides, nearly touching as the lift began its ascent. The atmosphere was electric; every breath seemed to carry a silent promise. She watched the floor numbers illuminate one by one, each bringing her closer to something she couldn't name but deeply craved.

As colleagues exited at various floors, the space around them opened up. Isabella fought the urge to move closer, her fingers tingling with the desire to touch him, to reaffirm the connection they had forged when they were entwined in the early hours, their hunger for each other undeniable. She could almost feel the warmth radiating from him, the memory sending a shiver through her. But she couldn't close the space between them. Not here. Not with others around.

Then, as the last of the passengers departed, only the two of them remained.

The lift continued its steady climb, but neither of them spoke. Isabella felt the tension rising, but Zach remained unmoving as the numbers ascended. He said nothing, didn't even glance her way, and the silence stretched, growing heavier with each passing second.

Why wasn't he saying anything?

Her thoughts spiralled, confusion mingling with tension. She stole a sideways glance at him, but his focus remained on the panel, his expression calm and unreadable. The pressure became unbearable, and she could no longer hold back. Without turning her head, she spoke softly, her voice laden with emotion.

"Last night was... unforgettable."

Her words hung between them like a delicate thread.

Zach blinked, a slight furrow appearing on his brow as he slowly turned to face her. "Last night?" he repeated, his tone genuinely puzzled. "Why? What happened?"

Isabella felt her heart lurch—not with excitement, but with a sinking dread. She stared straight ahead, her mind scrambling to make sense of his response. Surely he was teasing, playing coy? But there was no hint of mischief in his eyes—only confusion.

"You... you don't remember?" she stammered. Turning to look at him fully, her eyes searched his face. "Last night. This morning. Us."

His confusion deepened. He tilted his head, concern edging into his gaze. "Isabella, I've been here all night," he said carefully. "I've been working in the lab. Are you feeling okay? You look... pale."

The floor seemed to drop away beneath her feet, her stomach twisting as if the ground had opened up, ready to swallow her. He couldn't be serious.

"I think this is your floor," Zach added gently, his eyes indicating the open lift doors she hadn't noticed. He looked back at her with a mix of bemusement and mild concern.

"Oh," she murmured, dazed. "Yes. Sorry."

Her legs carried her forward on autopilot, her mind a whirlwind of disbelief and hurt. Stepping into the corridor, she turned just as the doors began to close. Zach's eyes remained on hers, his expression that of someone attempting to decipher her words, her meaning, her evident confusion.

Why was he pretending? Why act as if last night hadn't happened? Was this some kind of game? Or worse... was she losing her grip on reality?

The doors slid shut with a soft hiss, leaving her standing alone, staring at her faint reflection in the polished metal.

She stood there, motionless, words failing her.

15 – ECHOES OF ANOTHER LIFE

" While time marches forward, our memories wander through the corridors of the past."

Hotel Napoleon, Boulevard de Waterloo 33, 1000 Brussels – *10:00 PM, March 6*

James sat alone in the dim glow of his hotel room, the impact of his actions pressing down like an unbearable burden. The city outside hummed with life—the distant murmur of traffic seeping through the windows—but within these walls, silence reigned. His gaze rested on his phone, the dark screen reflecting the void that had opened between him and Isabella.

He had returned from yet another business trip, hoping for change, but nothing had improved. Their conversations—if they could still be called that—were stilted and awkward. A chill had settled in her voice, a distance widening more each day. He had tried to fix it, but deep down, he knew.

He was losing her.

And it all seemed to circle back to Zach.

James knew little about the man—only that his name had slipped from Isabella's lips in her sleep. But the way she had uttered it, the tenderness in her voice, haunted him. She'd spoken with a softness he hadn't heard in years, a passion that cut deeper than he cared to admit. He longed for the security she offered him. The irony of his repeated infidelities lost to him, though.

With a frustrated sigh, he ruffled his hair, pushing back against the headboard. A half-empty glass of whisky stood on the nightstand, his sole companion in this bleak moment. Emotions had never been his strong suit; he was practical, methodical. But love? Love was messy, unpredictable. And now, it was slipping through his fingers like sand.

The sound of someone at the door jolted him from his brooding. His heart leapt, a spark of hope igniting despite himself. Could it be her? Had Isabella come to mend whatever had fractured between them?

He stood swiftly, crossed the room, and opened the door.

But it wasn't her.

Davina stood there, poised and composed. Wickedly dressed as always, her black coat draped over her shoulders like a mantle of authority. The sight of her filled him with unease.

"Davina," he said flatly, masking his disappointment. "What brings you here?"

She offered a small, knowing smile, stepping inside without waiting for an invitation. "I was in the neighbourhood," she said smoothly, her gaze sweeping the room as if appraising it. "Thought I'd see how you're holding up."

He closed the door behind her, unease crawling over him. He knew Davina well enough to recognise that her visits were never casual; she always had an agenda.

"I'm fine," he replied tersely, moving back toward the bed. "Just tired."

She studied his face before settling into the chair by the window, crossing her legs with deliberate grace. "You don't look fine."

He didn't respond, unwilling to engage in her games. Yet her presence filled the room with a tension he couldn't shake.

"You know," she continued, her tone light but edged with intent, "I've been thinking about your situation—with Isabella."

His jaw tightened at the mention of his wife's name. He turned away, unwilling to fall into whatever manipulation Davina was planning.

"It's none of your business," he said quietly.

She chuckled softly. "Perhaps not. But it's clearly affecting you. You're distracted, unfocused. And we both know how dangerous that can be in our line of work."

His fists clenched at her insinuation, anger simmering below the surface. "What is it you want, Davina?"

She didn't answer immediately. Instead, she rose and approached him, her eyes tightening as she studied him. "You don't have to pretend with me, James. I understand what it's like to feel powerless—to watch something you cherish slip away."

Her words hit harder than expected, but he kept his expression guarded, his eyes lowered. Thoughts of Isabella, of Zach, of the life unravelling before him swirled chaotically in his mind.

"I don't need your advice," he muttered.

Davina raised an eyebrow, her demeanour unchanged. "No? Because from where I'm standing, you could use some assistance. You want Isabella back, don't you?"

His breath caught, heart pounding. Of course he wanted her back. But the admission felt heavy, laden with frustration and guilt.

"I'm not sure that's possible anymore," he confessed.

Her gaze softened slightly, though a calculating gleam remained. "It is possible. But you need to stop waiting for things to mend themselves. You need to take control."

He looked up, scepticism mingling with curiosity. "And how exactly am I supposed to do that?"

Her smile widened, but it didn't reach her eyes. "There are ways to influence outcomes. You know that. The choices we make—nothing is immutable."

James stared at her, her words sinking in. She wasn't merely discussing his relationship; she was hinting at something far more profound. Yet the idea of seizing control—of having a chance to win Isabella back—was intoxicating.

"What are you suggesting?" he asked his suspicion giving way to hope.

Davina leaned closer, her voice conspiratorial. "You're not seeing the full picture. Isabella and Zach... they've been spending time together. More than just during work hours."

He blinked, taken aback. "What?"

She slipped her phone from her pocket, swiping through images before handing it to him. "I had my suspicions. These were taken earlier this week."

James's heart sank as he stared at the photos: Isabella and Zach standing close, their body language intimate. One image showed Zach's hand resting on the small of her back as they left a café.

"I didn't want to believe it either," Davina said, her tone feigning sympathy. "But she's slipping away, James. If you don't act now, it'll be too late."

A surge of anger coursed through him. "What am I supposed to do?"

Davina's eyes gleamed as she stepped even closer, her voice low and persuasive. "Go to your apartment. Obtain her research. I have a hunch there's more at play than a mere office romance. Something bigger is unfolding, and I need to know what it is."

He regarded her warily. "Why are you interested in her research?"

Her smile turned enigmatic. "Let's just say there are influential parties keen on the technologies she and Zach are developing. You'll be doing us both a favour."

James hesitated, doubts clouding his mind. Yet the anger, the jealousy, the fear of losing Isabella—of her choosing Zach over him—spurred him on.

"And if I do this?" he asked, steadier now, him resolve briefly surfacing.

Davina's eyes never left his as she replied, "Then I'll help you win her back. Whatever it takes." Her fingers lightly touched his arm, her final words a silken promise. "Together, we'll ensure Zach Mondori doesn't take what's yours."

And you can have much more than he could ever dream of too."

Her smile was sharp, like the glint of a blade. Without another word, she reached for the clasp of her coat and let it slip to the floor with the soft whisper of fabric. Beneath, she wore nothing but exquisite black lingerie, the delicate lace accentuating every curve.

James's breath caught as she moved towards him, each step deliberate, imbued with intention. Reaching the bed, her gaze locked onto his, she picked up his glass of whisky from the nightstand. In one fluid motion, she drained it entirely. The thrill of the moment removed any remaining hesitation from his mind. This was the life he wanted, regardless of the risks or consequences.

Setting the empty tumbler aside, she knelt upon the bed, her movements slow and sensual as she closed the distance between them. Her hands glided lightly over the sheets as she leaned closer, a wicked smile playing on her lips.

The feel of her lace against his skin, the heady scent she

wore filling his lungs, were all it took to push him to the point of capitulation.

"Ready to play my game then?" she purred, her voice a low murmur. She brought her lips near his ear, her warmth of her touch against his skin.

He met her eyes, a storm of emotions swirling within him. The path she offered was fraught with uncertainty, but the promise of regaining what he'd lost was a potent lure, as was the moment itself.

"Yes," he answered firmly.

Davina's smile deepened, satisfaction evident.

"Then let's begin."

16 – BEYOND THE ILLUSION

"Half the truth is often a great lie."

The Dolce Vita Café, 2A Kensington High Street, London W8 4PT - 12:30 PM, March 7

Isabella wandered along the path leading to "La Dolce Vita," the quaint café where she'd once met Maggie and Zach. She suspected it might be his haven, but today she simply needed a place that held the joy of a cherished memory—a spot where she could contemplate her life, her strained relationship with James, and the burgeoning feelings she harboured for Zach.

Choosing a table outside beneath the striped awning that cast dappled shadows, she settled into her chair and exhaled a long, slow breath. Her mind replayed the moment in the lift—the confusion, the awkwardness, and the embarrassment sweeping over her. How could she have been so certain of that night when he seemed to have no recollection of it at all?

"Un espresso doppio, per favore," she told the waiter when he appeared. She mustered a polite smile, though inside her thoughts tumbled, unresolved and disjointed. What was happening to her? And how could it be connected to the work they were immersed in?

Enjoying the view of the gardens, she watched children chasing each other across the grass and couples strolling hand in hand. Sadness stirred within. She recalled a time when she cared deeply for James. He used to be dependable—a good husband and a devoted father to their daughter, Katie. But over time, things had changed. But over time, things had changed. As he had grown tired of their routine, seeking other distractions and affection, a restlessness had taken root in her soul. Whispers of untold adventures and passions yet to be fulfilled, slowly growing louder.

Her gaze fell on her left hand. She had put away her wedding ring after their last argument, and though it was a small act, the absence of that simple band felt like a silent admission—an acknowledgment that perhaps things were not as they should be.

Her reverie was interrupted by a familiar voice. "Is this seat taken?"

Looking up, Isabella felt a flutter as Zach stood before her, a small smile appearing and the now familiar rush of nerves. She gestured to the empty chair. "No, please, sit."

He settled across from her, his eyes studying her intently. "I wasn't sure you'd want to see me after... well, after the lift incident."

She felt a blush creeping up her neck but managed a light laugh. "It was... unexpected, to say the least."

"I can imagine," Zach replied in amusement. "I've been thinking about it, actually. It's been bothering me that I might have said something to upset you."

"You didn't," she assured him quickly, her eyes dropping to her cup. "It wasn't anything you said. It's just... I had this dream—or rather, I guess it must have been a dream—about us. About you and me. It felt so real, like it actually happened, and then in the lift..." She trailed off, uncertain how to continue without sounding unhinged.

Zach edged closer, a gentle smile softening his features. "Please, go on."

She hesitated, her fingers lightly tracing the rim of her cup. "In the dream, we were... close. Really close. It felt so vivid, like I was there. When I saw you in the lift, I was convinced you knew. But when you didn't, I just felt... foolish."

His expression softened, absorbing her words with a quiet understanding. "Isabella, you're not foolish. And, honestly, I don't think it's not as strange as it sounds."

Her eyes met his, curiosity mingling with a touch of relief. "You really think so?"

He shook his head, smiling gently. "Absolutely. Look,

we're messing with quantum entanglement—playing with time and space in ways that defy what most people can even begin to imagine. Who's to say that what you experienced wasn't real on some level? It might even be connected to everything we're working on."

She blinked, taken aback. The déjà vu was undeniable; she'd already had this exact conversation—in her dream. With a mix of amusement and disbelief, she shook her head. "See? I knew it. We've talked about this before! So, do you really think it's possible? I wasn't just imagining it?"

Zach's eyes opened wide. "Seriously? We've had this exact conversation before? That's... wow." He leaned in slightly, his tone light but edged with something deeper. "Well, it's definitely possible. We're tinkering with forces that warp reality in ways we don't fully grasp yet. Maybe what you experienced was... I don't know, a sneak peek into another timeline—a little cross-dimensional eavesdropping." He flashed her a playful wink. "Who's to say we didn't share a few stolen moments we weren't supposed to see?"

Isabella couldn't help but laugh, her earlier embarrassment dissolving in the warmth of his humour. "I don't know why, but that actually makes sense. I couldn't shake the feeling that something *physical* had happened between us."

Zach relaxed into his chair, his gaze unwavering. "I don't know what happened in your dream, Isabella, but I'd be lying if I said I hadn't thought about you too."

A rush of warmth coursed through her. "You have?"

He smiled—a warm, genuine smile that sent a flutter through her. "Yes. You're intelligent, witty, and... well, rather unforgettable."

She felt a flush rise to her cheeks and looked away, attempting to conceal the effect his words had on her. She wasn't accustomed to feeling this way—desired, appreciated. It was a welcome change to the strained silences that now filled her home life.

They sat quietly, unmoving. Finally, Zach interrupted the silence. "I'm glad we talked about this. I wouldn't want you to feel uncomfortable around me, especially when we're working on something as significant as the Quantum Bridge."

She met his eyes, gratitude evident. "I don't feel uncomfortable anymore. Just... intrigued."

"Intrigue is good," he replied with a grin. "It keeps life interesting."

Isabella couldn't help but laugh, the tension easing away. "You're right about that."

The waiter returned with Zach's latte, placing it gently on the table. He took a sip before speaking again. "So, where do we go from here?"

She reflected at length, possibilities swirling in her mind. "I suppose we continue working together and see where it leads."

"Sounds like a plan," Zach agreed, his excitement easy to read. "But for the record, if you dream about me again, feel free to share. I'd be curious to hear how it unfolds."

She laughed lightly, the sound genuine. "I'll keep that in mind."

They finished their coffee in comfortable silence, the awkwardness of their earlier encounter left behind. As they stood to leave, Zach lightly touched her arm, his fingers brushing her skin ever so briefly. The simple gesture sent a spark of warmth coursing through her.

"See you at the lab tomorrow?" he asked casually, though his eyes hinted at something deeper.

"Yes," she replied, her heart still racing from his touch. "See you tomorrow."

Walking away from the café, heading back towards the office, Isabella's mind was no longer clouded with confusion. Instead, it was filled with the flicker of something new—something uncertain, yet brimming with promise.

**

The Keane residence, Russell Square Mansions, 12 Russell Square, Bloomsbury, London, WC1B 5BG - 11:00 PM, March 7

Later that night, as she lay in an empty, loveless bed, Isabella stared up at the ceiling. Her thoughts drifted back to the café, replaying every detail of her conversation with Zach. There was an undeniable connection, a spark that defied all logic. And a sense of déjà vu. A fleeting memory of their conversation from another time flashed by. Had this happened before?

Sleep eventually claimed her, but her dreams were fragmented—a labyrinth of corridors, flashes of blinding light, and always those piercing eyes watching her with an intensity that both unsettled and captivated her.

Her dreams whispered to her in the darkness.

"Who are you, really?"

17 – SEIZE THE MOMENT

"We are never deceived; we deceive ourselves."

Obsidian Industries, The Tower, 1 St. George Wharf, Vauxhall, London SW8 2DA – 11:58 AM, March 14

Davina sat poised at her sleek, polished desk, her fingers drumming lightly on the surface as she listened intently to the voice on the other end of the line. The office was bathed in a subdued glow, illuminated only by the soft light of her computer screen and the shimmering city lights beyond the bullet-proof glass. Crossing one leg elegantly over the other, the tap of her stiletto echoed rhythmically against the leg of the desk.

"Is it done?" she inquired, her voice crisp and authoritative.

"Yes, ma'am," came the prompt reply. "Everything's been arranged exactly as you specified. The lingerie package is on the bed, the handwritten note in the drawer—it looks convincingly like something Zach would send."

A slow, satisfied smile curved Davina's lips as she reclined slightly, eyes glinting with calculated pleasure. "Excellent. And the surveillance devices? Are they positioned as required?"

"All set. Once James plays his part, we'll have access to every corner of Isabella's home."

"Splendid," she purred. "Ensure James remains none the wiser."

Through the receiver, she could hear the operatives moving efficiently, likely gathering their equipment and preparing to exit the premises. They were professionals—meticulous and discreet. Davina had always surrounded herself with the best; even the finest, however, required precise direction. Mastery was, after all, in the minutiae.

She clicked the pen in her hand absentmindedly, her thoughts drifting to the next phase of her design. James was malleable—a jealous husband desperate to reclaim control over a life slipping through his fingers. Perfect. He needn't comprehend the full scope; he simply needed to act, propelled by the carefully crafted deceptions she had laid before him. With this fabricated "evidence," he would have every reason to believe his worst fears were reality—that Isabella was drifting away, straight into Zach's embrace.

Her smile broadened, triumph written all over her face. It was almost too easy, too effortless.

"Leave everything exactly as you found it," she instructed, her tone cool and commanding. "I don't want her suspecting a thing."

"Understood. We're leaving now."

"Good. I expect a full report once you're clear."

Ending the call, Davina allowed her gaze to linger on the glittering skyline before turning back to her desk. A small, framed photograph caught her eye—one of the few personal touches in her otherwise minimalist office. It depicted a younger version of herself, standing proudly in her first laboratory. For a fleeting moment, her smile faded as old memories stirred—a whisper of the person she once was. But she dismissed the sentiment. The past was a tether she had long since severed. Power was her currency now, and she was within touching distance of seizing it in full.

With a deliberate sigh, she opened a thick, black folder resting on her desk. Inside lay comprehensive dossiers on the Quantum Bridge project, Zach, Isabella, James, Ted, and even Maggie. Each was a piece on her chessboard, but it was Isabella who posed the most significant threat. Brilliant, resourceful—and regrettably for Davina—becoming a variable that eluded complete control.

That's why this scheme was imperative. Isabella needed to be destabilised, her footing uncertain. And James... he would be the unwitting instrument of her downfall.

Her phone flashed, catching her attention. A message regarding James illuminated the screen: *Flight plans changed. He's on his way.*

Her smile returned, slow and calculated. Everything was aligning perfectly. She typed a succinct response: *Good.*

***

The boardroom at Obsidian Industries stood in marked contrast to the clinical precision of Daystrom Biotech's laboratories. Here, opulence reigned—rich mahogany panelling, artful lighting, and an air thick with unspoken ambition. Davina presided at the head of the expansive, gleaming table, her fingers steepled thoughtfully. Beyond the vast windows, the Vauxhall skyline was shrouded in a misty veil of London rain.

Her inner circle—the select few entrusted with executing her intricate plans—were assembled around her. Each had been chosen for their unwavering efficiency and a shared ruthlessness. The atmosphere was taut, their attention exclusively given to Davina. They understood that when she convened them, the stakes were nothing less than monumental, their careers, suspended by a thread, ready to be severed at the slightest indiscretion.

Adjusting her posture with composed elegance, Davina surveyed the room before speaking. "The International

Science Awards take place next week in Zurich," she began, her voice smooth yet resonant. "Daystrom intends to unveil more than just their latest findings—they plan to showcase the Quantum Bridge to the global scientific community. This is their moment to ascend as the foremost research institution worldwide. We must be prepared to seize this opportunity and turn it to our advantage."

She allowed a moment for her words to permeate. "Our primary objective," she continued, "is to engineer a failure so profound that Daystrom's reputation crumbles irreparably. They must be exposed as unfit leaders in technological innovation."

A man seated to her left—slender, with keen, hawk-like features—raised a hand. "And what of Zach Mondori? He's pivotal to their endeavours."

"Precisely," Davina affirmed. "Our secondary objective is to obliterate Zach's professional standing. He must become untouchable in the industry, leaving him with no recourse but to turn to us. His fall from grace will be swift and absolute."

She gestured toward a screen that illuminated with detailed information on the Quantum Bridge project. "Our third goal is to secure the technology itself. With Daystrom discredited, Obsidian will emerge as the sole entity capable of harnessing and advancing the

Quantum Bridge. It will be mine to command."

The slender man interjected once more. "And how do you propose to deal with Zach?"

Davina's gaze sharpened. "Zach will be the fulcrum of this operation. We'll ensure there is a confrontation involving him, Isabella, and James—a scenario crafted for maximum impact. He'll be with Isabella in a suitable setting—not overtly scandalous, but enough to provoke James into a rash response. That will ignite the scandal we require."

Evelyn arched an eyebrow. "And if the media catches wind?"

"That's precisely the intention," Davina replied, her smile tinged with cold satisfaction. "Our operatives will be in place to capture everything. The media will revel in the downfall of Zach Mondori amidst the grandeur of the Science Awards. Should it be necessary, we'll facilitate the leak of compromising footage. The ensuing media storm will not only annihilate his career but also cast Daystrom into disrepute."

Evelyn folded her hands, her gaze measured. "And James?"

Davina's eyes glinted. "James is blinded by his own insecurities and jealousy. He will accept the reality we present. By the time any doubts surface—if they ever do

—it will be far too late."

"A low chuckle emanated from the man beside her. "You've anticipated every variable."

Davina inclined her head modestly. "Naturally. Precision is paramount. This operation must appear as a natural cascade of events—a collision of egos and flawed judgments. In executing this plan, we will eliminate three of Daystrom's key assets. When the dust settles, Obsidian will stand unrivalled, the Quantum Bridge firmly within our grasp."

A murmur of assent rippled through the room as each member absorbed the purpose of their roles. They were acutely aware that perfection was non-negotiable; the slightest error could unravel everything.

"I expect real-time updates at every juncture," Davina concluded, her tone brooking no dissent. "This is our defining moment. We cannot afford any miscalculations. The Science Awards will be our stage, and we will control every act."

Rising gracefully, she signalled the meeting's end. The team dispersed with purposeful strides, each intent on fulfilling their part with exacting precision. As the door closed behind the last of them, Davina turned once more to the vast expanse of the cityscape, a cool serenity washing over her. The intricate web she had woven was taut, every thread poised for the final pull. She mused silently.

"Success is fleeting, only power endures."

18 – SOLVING THE PUZZLE

" What seems like magic to some is simply science to others"

The Keane residence, Russell Square Mansions, 12 Russell Square, Bloomsbury, London, WC1B 5BG – 06:58 AM, March 22

Her apartment radiated an unusual warmth that evening, the air thick with a blend of relief and underlying tension. Workplace conversations had drifted from the challenges at Daystrom, lightening in the mellow glow of softly lit lamps. Isabella had invited Maggie, Zach, and Ted over for drinks, their usual professional demeanour softened by a shared sense of achievement. The enigma of the Quantum Bridge was beginning to reveal itself, and the magnitude of their discoveries had become a new talking point.

Isabella poured another glass of wine, her hand steady despite the tumult of emotions swirling within. She handed the glass to Maggie, who accepted it with a nod, her keen eyes surveying the room as though unable to fully relax. Zach reclined on the sofa, legs stretched out, shirt sleeves rolled up, a couple of buttons undone —a picture of ease that belied the frisson simmering between him and Isabella. Their exchanged glances carried unspoken words—something unacknowledged but palpably present.

Ted stood near the expansive windows, his eyes toward the skyline, hands tucked into his pockets. "Well," he began, breaking the comfortable silence, "we've got the data to back it up now. The surges are directly linked to the visions. If we stabilize those power spikes, perhaps we can prevent... whatever else is seeping through."

Maggie sipped her wine thoughtfully. "The visions are genuine, aren't they? Not mere hallucinations but actual possibilities from alternate realities."

Zach nodded slowly. "Real enough. We're glimpsing lives where different choices were made. The bridge is doing more than we anticipated—it's revealing what might have been and destabilizing everything in the process, including..." He hesitated, his gaze meeting Isabella's once more. "Including people's lives."

Isabella's heart skipped a beat. She didn't need him to elaborate. Her dreams—or rather, visions—had been so vivid. Moments with Zach, intimate conversations that felt more authentic than anything she'd experienced in years with James. Knowing they could be more than fantasies was intoxicating.

Before she could respond, the sound of the front door opening caught her attention. Moments later, Katie's voice echoed from the hallway. "Mum?"

Katie, Isabella's teenage daughter, peeked into the living room, her eyes sweeping over the assembled adults. A mischievous grin tugged at her lips. "Wow, Mum, is this a work meeting or something else? Didn't realise you were hosting a party tonight."

Isabella rolled her eyes, a smile breaking through. "Katie, these are just colleagues. We've been working on something important."

Katie gave Zach a pointed look, her grin widening. "Uh-huh, colleagues. Sure."

Zach chuckled, clearly amused by her cheekiness. "Strictly work, I promise."

"Whatever you say," Katie teased, then turned to her mother. "I'm heading out with friends—sleepover. Don't wait up."

"Be careful," Isabella called after her, but Katie was already disappearing down the hallway, laughter trailing behind her.

The door clicked shut, leaving an abrupt silence that felt suddenly charged.

Ted cleared his throat, attempting to steer the focus back. "We've confirmed what's happening, but we're still left with the pressing question—what does this mean for us and the project? What else might come through that bridge? What might we uncover?"

Zach leaned forward, hands clasped. "It's bigger than we ever imagined, Ted. The implications are immense. We could be seeing alternate realities, each one invading our own. We need to contain this before something irreversible occurs."

Isabella took a measured sip of her wine, Zach's words resonating deeply. She recalled the moments that had flashed through her mind—the feel of his touch, how he spoke her name in the twilight hours. These weren't mere dreams; they were glimpses into a life she hadn't lived but could have.

"These visions," she began softly, "if they're from other realities... does that mean..."

Zach turned to her, his gaze gentle yet serious. "It means that what you saw—what we've all been seeing—is possible. In another timeline, those events are real. The choices we didn't make, paths we didn't follow—they're out there, unfolding alongside this version of events."

She struggled to process the words. The room seemed to shrink, the endless possibilities confounding her. She looked toward Zach, her thoughts spiralling. Could she allow herself to desire that life? The one she'd glimpsed with him? Her marriage to James was already fraying, unravelling before her eyes.

Setting her glass down, she noticed a slight tremor in her hand. "So, what do we do now?"

Maggie, who had been observing the exchange with a distant yet knowing expression, interjected. "Now, we work on halting the surges or at least containing them. We can't risk alternate realities bleeding into ours. It's not just a threat to the project—it's *life-threatening* to all of us."

Ted nodded in agreement. "We need to approach this with utmost seriousness. Stabilise the power inputs, slow down our testing if necessary, and focus on preventing the bridge from destabilizing further."

As the discussion continued, Isabella's thoughts drifted back to Zach's words. *In another timeline, those events are real.* She felt as if she stood on the brink of something monumental—both in her work and personal life. But which path should she choose?

Amidst the conversation, an unsettling feeling nagged at her, as though Davina's shadow loomed—unseen yet ever-present, waiting for the opportune moment to strike.

***

As the evening progressed and wine glasses emptied, Ted glanced at his watch and cleared his throat. "I've got an early start tomorrow," he announced, pushing back his chair. "Need to begin preparations for the demonstration the board has scheduled in Zurich at month's end."

Maggie seized the moment. "Ted, could I hitch a ride? It's on your way, and I'd rather avoid the underground tonight."

He nodded, retrieving his coat. "Sure. Let's go."

As they moved towards the door, Maggie lingered briefly, turning to Zach with a subtle smile. Leaning in, she whispered, "Carpe diem, Zach. Don't be foolish."

He blinked, momentarily taken aback, but said nothing. His eyes followed her as she kissed Isabella lightly on the cheek. "Make the right choices this time," she murmured, her words laden with meaning that Isabella couldn't ignore.

With that, Maggie and Ted departed, leaving Isabella and Zach alone in the now-quiet apartment. An unspoken charge filled the air, the earlier lively conversation fading into a distant backdrop. Isabella wandered to the kitchen island, her fingers gliding over the cool granite as she poured herself another glass of wine, a subtle tremor betraying her inner turmoil.

Zach joined her, standing close enough that their arms nearly touched. His proximity sent a warm rush through her, awakening feelings that had lain dormant for too long. She handed him a glass, their fingers brushing lightly as he accepted.

They stood in companionable silence, sipping their drinks. The kitchen seemed smaller, the space between them fraught with possibilities. Zach glanced sideways at her, speaking with gentle uncertainty. "About what Maggie said earlier... do you think she meant...?"

Isabella's heart raced, aware of his gaze upon her. "I think she knows more than she lets on," she replied softly, though they were alone.

He chuckled. "She usually does."

Their eyes met, the air crackling with an undeniable electricity. The pull between them was strong, the temptation of an uncharted path beckoning. Isabella's mind danced between the choices before her—the life she'd glimpsed in visions, the reality that could be if she dared to reach out.

Zach set his glass down, hesitating before gently taking her hand. "Isabella..."

This was it—the moment she had longed for, the one that haunted her thoughts in quiet hours. Her heart pounded, her mind urging her to embrace a choice she had been too afraid to make. With a soft, unsteady breath, she set her glass beside his, her fingers trembling as they reached up to rest against his cheek.

They lingered, suspended in time, silently searching for permission. Then, as if pulled by a force he could no longer resist, Zach closed the distance. His lips met hers in a kiss that was both tender and inevitable—a quiet collision of longing that felt both new and profoundly familiar, as if their paths had always been leading to this moment. It began softly, a delicate brush of lips, but quickly deepened, releasing the torrent of emotions they had kept buried for far too long.

Isabella melted into his embrace, her fingers tangling in his hair as she surrendered to the moment. In a single movement, Zach pushed her gently but firmly against the cool granite of the kitchen island. She gasped softly, her hands instinctively moving behind her to steady herself.

As her palms pressed against the surface, she grazed something small and cold—her wedding ring. It began to roll, spinning slowly as if caught in time, before falling to the floor with a soft, delicate chime. The sound lingered briefly in the air as the ring rolled out of sight, unnoticed by either of them.

This was her choice—not a vision, not a dream, but real, tangible, and hers.

They parted just enough for their foreheads to touch, the enormity of what they'd just begun settling between them. But there was no regret, only a quiet certainty that this was where they were meant to be.

"I've fallen for you, Isabella," Zach whispered, his emotions laid bare. "I've been waiting for you since the beginning of time. And I never want to lose you, never let you go."

Her heart swelled, warmth blooming within her like a long-forgotten light. She smiled gently, her hand caressing his cheek. "I've been waiting for this my whole life too." she whispered back.

Their lips met again, and this time, there was no hesitation, no turning back.

That night, for the first time in what felt like forever, Isabella sensed the possibility of something new—a choice that was hers alone to make. For her happiness, for the life she had only glimpsed in her dreams. A way of being that, at last, might be within her reach.

She just had to make the most important choice.

19 – SHORT TERM GAIN

"Temptation's allure is captivating, but every desire demands its price."

Grand Hotel du Lac, Talstrasse 33, 8001 Zurich - 7:20 PM, March 27

James stepped off the plane, weariness settling deep into his bones. His work schedule had been abruptly altered, necessitating an unscheduled stop in Zurich. His last conversation with Isabella had been strained, filled with a silence that spoke louder than words. He had hoped to hear from her by the time he landed, but his phone remained stubbornly silent.

At the hotel, the receptionist checked his details and handed him a small, folded note. "This was left for you by another guest," she said with a polite smile.

He unfolded it. The handwriting was unfamiliar, but the message was clear:

Meet me at the bar. Davina.

James glanced around the opulent atrium, his gaze settling on the sleek bar where Davina Drake sat perched gracefully on a high stool. Clad in a crimson dress that accentuated her lithe figure, she exuded a magnetic allure—a dangerous blend of confidence and charm that set him on edge. He could sense the impending clouds gathering.

Collecting his thoughts, he made his way over, her eyes meeting his as he approached. "Now what is it, Davina?" he asked bluntly, the fatigue and irritation seeping through. Her unexpected presence unnerved him; the last thing he desired was to become entangled in her intricate games.

Davina offered a sly smile, her lips curving in a way that hinted at hidden intentions. "I've been waiting patiently for you to get here. Why not freshen up first, James?" she suggested, her fingers brushing lightly against his sleeve. "You look like you could use a drink, and we have much to discuss."

He hesitated, her steady gaze challenging him. With a curt nod, he turned and headed toward the lift, feeling a reluctant resignation to circumstances slipping beyond his control.

In his room, James tossed his suitcase onto the bed and strode to the window, the city shimmering against the night sky. He retrieved a miniature of branded alcohol from the minibar, pouring it into a glass and staring at his reflection before swallowing it in a single gulp. The liquid burned but did little to soothe his frayed nerves.

His phone buzzed—a message, but not from Isabella. Their last exchange replayed in his mind: terse, distant, a gap between them seemingly unbridgeable.

Setting the phone aside, he took a hot shower and changed into fresh clothes more suited to the evening. The mirror reflected a man who seemed a stranger to himself—a weary traveller lost in his own life.

Steeling himself, he left the room and returned to the bar.

Davina descended from her stool with an almost feline grace as he approached. Her dress caught the ambient light, drawing his gaze despite himself. Without preamble, she pressed a brief, unexpected kiss to his cheek, her perfume enveloping him—a scent both enticing and unsettling.

"Shall we go somewhere more interesting?" she suggested smoothly.

Before he could protest, she linked her arm through his and guided him toward the entrance. Part of him wanted to pull away, to extricate himself from whatever this was, but a weariness—compounded by frustration and a touch of masculine curiosity—held him in place. He allowed her to lead him through the lobby and outside to a waiting car.

The limo glided through Zurich's illuminated streets.

Davina sat beside him, the silence palpable. Her proximity was disconcerting; he could feel the subtle energy she emanated—a calculated poise and underlying intent.

"What is this about?" James finally asked, his tone guarded.

Davina turned to face him. "All in good time," she replied enigmatically. "I have something to show you."

***

Velvet Shadows, Bogenstrasse 22, 8002 Zurich - 08:10 PM, March 27

They drove for what felt like an eternity before the car pulled up beside an unassuming building in a quiet district of the city. There were no signs or markings —just a discreet entrance leading down a short flight of steps. The dim lighting and sleek exterior belied the decadence that awaited inside.

Davina exited first, offering him her hand. "Trust me," she said softly.

He hesitated but followed her lead. Inside, the space opened into an elegant lounge adorned with subtle lighting and understated décor. The atmosphere was refined—the murmur of quiet conversations blending with soft music and the scent of expensive perfumes. It was a place that exuded exclusivity and opulence.

She guided him to a secluded corner where a low table was set with crystal glasses. A waiter appeared promptly, and Davina ordered a distinguished single malt for them both. As the amber liquid was poured, she raised her glass, her eyes meeting his over the rim. "To unexpected encounters," she toasted.

James took a measured sip, its warmth spreading through him. The decadent atmosphere seemed to close in around him—the low murmur of conversation and music creating a heady mix. He struggled to maintain his composure.

"What's the purpose of this meeting, Davina?" he asked, striving to keep calm.

"Relax, James," Davina whispered in his ear, her voice warm and teasing. "You look tense." Her body pressed lightly against his as they sank further into the plush leather seating.

She settled back in her chair, her gaze steady on him. "Our last conversation keeps coming back to me. There's a lot going on—things that could benefit both our interests."

He frowned slightly. "I'm not sure I follow."

James shifted uneasily, his eyes darting around the

room. A waiter appeared almost instantly, as if summoned by an invisible signal. Davina gestured for fresh drinks. A second glass was placed in front of James, and before he could say a word, Davina raised her own glass, her eyes gleaming in the dim light.

She tilted her head, her expression softening further. "Isabella's work with the Quantum Bridge is groundbreaking, but it's also perilous. There are forces at play that she might not fully comprehend. She could be in danger."

A trace of concern crossed his face. "What do you know about Isabella's work?"

"More than you might expect," she replied smoothly. "And I believe you and I could help each other. Your connection to her puts you in a unique position."

James bristled. "If you think I'll spy on my wife again, you're mistaken. I'm done with that."

She sighed lightly. "James, I'm offering a mutual benefit. I can provide information that might help you understand what's pulling her away. Aren't you curious?"

He hesitated. "What are you suggesting?"

Davina leaned in slightly. "Simply that you keep your eyes open. Share any... unusual developments. In return,

I can offer you some... *insights*."

He regarded her warily. "What insights?"

With a slow, deliberate motion, she reached into her clutch bag. She placed a series of photographs on the table. With a flick of her fingers, she flipped the first photo over—two people locked in a passionate kiss, the intimacy undeniable. James stiffened, his eyes narrowing as his gaze darted between the image and Davina.

Without a word, she turned over the second photo. This one was more damning. A wave of jealousy and anger washed over him.

"These kind of insights," Davina said smoothly, her voice a silk thread of manipulation, "are what I can provide. And the benefit for you? Well, that depends on how you want to handle things."

She continued, pulling him deeper into the game she was playing. Her words both threatening and inviting at the same time. "Let's just say I have a vested interest in the outcomes of certain projects. Collaboration could be advantageous for us both."

Before James could process her words, she gestured toward the far side of the room. Two women approached, their eyes fixed on James with a predatory gleam. Davina made way, and they slid into the seats beside him—their presence impossible to dismiss, the air filled with temptation.

James's mind spun, the alcohol clouding his judgment. He found himself smiling, the tension from earlier ebbing away under the spotlight of their attention.

"I'll have to think about it," he finally replied.

"Of course," she agreed, her tone accommodating. "No pressure. Enjoy the evening."

Davina sank back in comfort, observing the scene with quiet satisfaction, sipping her drink as the women fawned over James, their flirtatious laughter drifting through the air. She watched him closely, noting the glazed look in his eyes, a blend of alcohol and the attention he was soaking in. A dark pleasure curled within her as the scene unfolded. Manipulating the emotions of others was a game she relished, a private indulgence that fed her need for control.

Eventually, satiated, she suggested they return to the hotel. The journey back was quiet, the city's nocturnal beauty passing by unnoticed.

At the hotel entrance, Davina placed a gentle hand on his arm. "Rest well, James. And let's keep what happened this evening to ourselves. We wouldn't want your wife to find out, would we?" Malice seeped into every word. "We'll speak again soon."

He nodded, not too tired to parse the meaning in her words. As he made his way to his room, he knew that he'd been drawn into a game whose rules he didn't fully understand.

Closing the door behind him, he sat on the bed. The room was silent, yet his mind swirled. Davina's threat lingered, entwined with his own doubts and fears about Isabella. The ticking of the clock grew louder in his ears, each second a reminder of time slipping away, pulling him further into an uncertain future.

Reaching for his phone, he considered calling his wife, the impulse to reconnect still flickering. But as his thumb hovered over her name, doubt crept in, and his resolve faltered. He set the phone down, its screen darkening, reflecting only his own indecision. Instead, he lay back, exhaustion finally claiming him. Outside, a storm was brewing, the distant rumble of thunder hinting at the line he was about to cross. As the final chime of midnight sounded, a sense of foreboding washed over him, chilling him with a single, cold certainty.

Whatever path he chose, there would be no turning back.

20 – ALL THAT GLITTERS

" We perceive only what our minds are willing to understand."

Lieben Park Hotel, Beethovenstrasse 24, 8002 Zürich - 1:30 PM, March 29

The Daystrom team arrived in Zurich amidst an atmosphere charged with anticipation. The city pulsed with energy as the International Science Awards drew together the world's most brilliant minds and influential figures. For the Daystrom group, this event represented more than mere recognition; they were shortlisted for the prestigious Research Prize and poised to unveil their groundbreaking work on the Quantum Bridge—a project that had intrigued the scientific community and was soon to be presented to the world.

As they checked into the hotel, Isabella's phone vibrated in her pocket. Glancing at the screen, she frowned upon seeing James's name flash before her eyes. With a deep sigh, she stepped aside from her colleagues and answered.

"James?" she said cautiously, striving to keep her voice steady.

"I'm here. In Zurich. I need to see you," came his slurred

reply.

She stiffened. "James, no. I'm here for work. I don't have time for this."

"Don't tell me what I can and can't do," he retorted sharply. "You don't get to shut me out like this. I know where you're staying."

A knot tightened in her stomach. She could almost smell the alcohol on his breath through the phone, the veneer of civility stripped away to reveal her raw heartache.

"James, you mustn't come—not like this. Do not come," she said firmly, each word measured to leave no room for misinterpretation.

There was a pause, followed by a bitter laugh. "You're with him, aren't you? That scientist—this is all for him, isn't it? You think I don't know?"

Her heart pounded, but she held her ground. "I'm not engaging in this conversation, James. Do not come, or it's over."

Without waiting for a response, she ended the call, her hand trembling as she slipped the phone back into her bag. Across the hotel lobby, the rest of the team chatted amiably, blissfully unaware of the storm brewing. Isabella closed her eyes momentarily, steadying herself.

Back in his hotel room, James stared at his phone, seething. Her rejection hit him like a sledgehammer. With a furious shout, he hurled his drink against the wall, watching as it shattered, liquid trailing down the patterned wallpaper. He stood amidst the wreckage, fists clenched. Jealousy, rage, and guilt churned within him. He wasn't about to let Isabella dismiss him—not tonight.

**

Kongresshaus Zürich, Gotthardstrasse 5, 8002 Zürich – 7:15 PM, March 29

That evening, a procession of sleek black vehicles lined the entrance of Zurich's most opulent venue. The International Science Awards had drawn the elite of the scientific world, and the air buzzed with excitement. Paparazzi thronged the entrance, camera flashes igniting the night as guests arrived.

A limousine door swung open, and out stepped Isabella, Ted, and Maggie. Elegantly attired, they epitomised sophistication. Isabella wore a midnight-red gown that shimmered under the lights, her hair swept back in soft waves. Maggie, equally resplendent in her attire, moved with poised grace, while Ted cut a dashing figure in his perfectly tailored tuxedo, his hand resting gently on Isabella's back as they navigated the throng of photographers.

Inside the grand hall, the Daystrom team mingled with fellow scientists, journalists, and industry leaders, exchanging cordial greetings. Their attention was, however, drawn to Davina and her entourage.

Davina Drake was impossible to overlook. Clad in a deliciously outrageous evening dress that skirted the boundaries of formality, she exuded a commanding presence. She approached with long, confident strides, a smile as sharp as the glint in her eyes.

"Darlings!" she purred upon reaching them, bestowing air kisses with calculated charm. "You all look marvellous tonight." Her tone was dulcet, yet beneath it lurked an unmistakable edge.

Zach had been at the venue since early morning, overseeing the final preparations for the Quantum Bridge's debut. Behind the main stage, the prototype stood gleaming and silent, awaiting its moment under the spotlight.

"You must be thrilled to be nominated for such a prestigious award," Davina continued, her sarcasm not lost to the group. "I hear the competition is particularly fierce this year."

Her eyes lingered on Isabella a fraction too long, something unsettling flickering within them.

"Best of luck," she added, her smile so saccharine it made Isabella's skin prickle.

Before anyone could respond, the master of ceremonies appeared, inviting guests to take their seats for dinner and the awards presentation. The Daystrom team settled at a large, round table near the stage, their nerves and excitement mingling with the glitz of the evening.

Zach completed the final checks on the Quantum Bridge, ensuring every connection was secure, every detail meticulously in place. Folding his lab coat neatly beside the device, he scanned the intricate machinery one last time, confirming all was ready. Satisfied, he locked the room, slipping the key card into the inner pocket of his tuxedo jacket. He adjusted his jacket and made his way to the main hall where the event was in full swing.

Joining his colleagues at the table, he looked effortlessly refined in his bespoke suit. Isabella couldn't help but notice, captivated by the contrast between his polished appearance and the dedicated scientist she knew so well. She wasn't alone; several guests cast admiring glances in his direction. Maggie observed quietly, a contented smile touching her lips. Perhaps this time, things would finally fall into place.

***

The lights dimmed as the ceremony commenced, Davina

observing from the shadows, the unseen puppeteer pulling unseen strings. Anticipation charged the atmosphere as each award was announced, recipients taking to the stage amidst enthusiastic applause.

Meanwhile, James arrived, stumbling slightly as he emerged from a taxi near the venue. Though dressed impeccably, his dishevelled appearance and odour of whisky betrayed his state. Security personnel at the entrance barred his way, citing strict protocols for late arrivals. Unwilling to be deterred, he became aggressive, a fight about to ensue, when two of Davina's personal security detail approached. After a brief exchange with the guards, one of them took James by the arm and escorted him inside, while the other composed a text message.

James was led through a labyrinth of corridors, his mind foggy but his determination unwavering. The men straightened his jacket, and he attempted to compose himself, the anger within him simmering. Isabella was somewhere inside, with Zach, and he intended to find them.

Amidst the clinking of champagne flutes, Davina's phone vibrated silently in her clutch. Casually, she retrieved it, her manicured fingers tapping the screen to read the message from her security detail:

James Keane is in the building.

A knowing smile curved her lips as she returned the phone to her bag. Everything was proceeding according to plan. Her gaze drifted to where Isabella and Zach were seated, blissfully unaware of the impending chaos. James had arrived right on schedule, a pawn in her meticulously crafted scheme. Now, she merely had to await the inevitable confrontation—a tempest of jealousy and upheaval that would tear through the delicate fabric of their lives. And she would be waiting, watching it unravel, ready to seize the advantage.

***

The ballroom buzzed with soft conversation, punctuated by the gentle clatter of silverware and glass. The Daystrom team sat at their table, offering a prime vantage point to observe the glittering assembly. Talk of the upcoming Quantum Bridge demonstration dominated their discourse, yet an undercurrent of personal intrigue wove through their interactions.

Zach and Isabella exchanged glances, their words professionally cordial, but their eyes conveyed unspoken sentiments. Isabella, radiant in a gown that accentuated her elegance, toyed subtly with the stem of her wine glass. "Are you feeling nervous about the demonstration?" she asked, her tone light yet tinged with playful challenge.

He smiled, meeting her gaze. "Nervous? Only if I thought

the bridge might fail," he replied, leaning in slightly. "But with you on the team, I have every confidence."

A faint blush coloured her cheeks, though she tried to mask it with a sip of wine. "Flattery won't save you if something goes awry," she teased, her eyes sparkling.

Maggie, seated beside Ted, observed their exchange with a knowing smile. "Ah, the charm of collaboration," she murmured, casting a wink in Ted's direction as he perused the schedule for the next day's showcase.

Ted glanced up, a slight furrow in his brow. "Collaboration? Let's keep our focus, shall we?" His attempt at maintaining professionalism elicited a chuckle from Maggie.

"Relax, Ted," she chided gently, nudging his arm. "It's a significant night; we can afford a moment's levity. Besides, you've reviewed the plan thoroughly."

He adjusted his tie, almost tempted to smile, or perhaps blush. " Let's just make sure everything goes smoothly." he insisted, though Maggie's light-heartedness eased his tension.

The atmosphere shifted as Davina approached their table, drawing their collective attention. Draped in a daringly elegant dress that clung to her form, she exuded an air of calculated allure. Her presence commanded the room.

"Well, well," she purred, leaning provocatively close to Zach, her eyes glittering. "I hear you're poised to astonish the world tomorrow." Her voice was sweet yet carried an undercurrent that set everyone slightly on edge.

Zach, momentarily taken aback, composed himself and offered a polite smile. "We're looking forward to it," he replied, though her proximity made him subtly shift in his seat.

Maggie raised an eyebrow, her disapproval barely concealed. Isabella regarded Davina coolly, ignoring the overtly affectionate display.

"Would you care to join us?" Ted offered, his tone courteous but lacking enthusiasm. He tugged at his collar, clearly uncomfortable under Davina's scrutiny.

She flashed a sultry smile. "How gracious of you, Ted," she said, standing upright with a graceful flourish. "But I have other matters requiring my attention." She trailed a manicured finger along the arm of a man standing nearby, his impeccable attire and stoic demeanour hinting at his role as more than just an escort.

The team watched as she leaned into him, her gesture possessive. "But I'll be sure to catch up with you all later," she added, her gaze flickering briefly to Zach with a hint of mischief. With that, she turned and melted into the throng, her companion following obediently.

Once she was out of earshot, Maggie rolled her eyes dramatically. "Davina, never one for subtlety." she remarked, swirling the wine in her glass.

Isabella nodded, her expression a mix of exasperation and relief. "I'm not sure which is more disconcerting—the way she dresses or the fact that she assumes we can't see through her façade."

Ted chuckled awkwardly, fiddling with his bow tie. "She certainly knows how to make an impression."

Maggie laughed, nudging him again. "Careful, Ted, or you might find yourself ensnared."

Zach, who had remained quiet, finally spoke, meeting Isabella's gaze. "She has a talent for commanding attention," he acknowledged.

Isabella smiled softly. "Let's hope that's the extent of her influence tonight."

As their conversation resumed, returning to the excitement of their work, Davina watched from a distance, her satisfaction clear to see. She brushed the side of her dress, and with a subtle motion, passed a small device to the man beside her, who pocketed it smoothly—a gesture so seamless it went unnoticed.

Every piece was in place. Time to play the end game.

21 – A JEALOUS DISTRACTION

"Jealousy corrodes the heart, while true love heals it; many confuse the two."

Kongresshaus Zürich Gotthardstrasse 5, 8002 Zürich – 08:50 PM March 29

The atmosphere in the grand hall buzzed with animated conversation as the second speech concluded and a twenty-minute interlude was announced for guests to mingle. Glasses clinked, soft laughter filled the air, and the aroma of exquisite cuisine lingered. Isabella stood beside Zach, engaged in dialogue with fellow attendees, her natural smile masking the unease beneath. It had been quite the journey to get here, and tonight everything needed to work out perfectly.

Meanwhile, just outside, James was being held back by Davina's associates, his mind dulled and distorted by alcohol. They kept him distracted just long enough for Davina's plan to unfold precisely as intended. As soon as the interlude was announced, they released him, pointing him toward the hall, a trail of jealousy already coursing through him.

With unsteady steps, he staggered inside, his gaze scanning the room until it locked onto Isabella, who stood close to Zach, the two conversing effortlessly among the guests. His blood boiled, the alcohol fuelling his frustration. He staggered forward, his unbuttoned jacket swinging wildly, as he jostled past guests who murmured in surprise and annoyance.

The commotion caught Isabella's attention first. She glanced up, her eyes widening as she saw James barrelling toward them, his face flushed with intoxicated anger. "James?" she whispered in disbelief, her body tensing as she instinctively moved closer to Zach.

Within moments, James was upon them, his movements clumsy but his intent unmistakable. "You!" he yelled, , his voice slurring but loud enough to draw every eye in the room. "Think you can steal my wife?"

Zach moved forward, palms raised in a placating gesture. "James, you're not thinking straight. Let's talk this through."

But James's anger flared unchecked. "Talk? Is that what you call it when you're sneaking around?" His voice carried across the room, silencing conversations and drawing whispers as phones began to appear, cameras recording the spectacle.

Davina watched from her vantage point, sipping her champagne, her satisfaction hidden behind a composed smile. Every detail, every emotion was playing out exactly as she'd planned.

"James, please stop!" Isabella pleaded, her voice shaking. "You're causing a scene."

He turned his fiery gaze on her. "And you! Lying to me, betraying me!" His words slurred, but the hurt in them was evident. "I gave you everything!"

Security personnel began moving through the crowd, alerted by the disturbance. Guests exchanged uneasy glances, whispers spreading.

"Let's step outside and discuss this privately," Zach suggested calmly, trying to deescalate the situation.

James sneered. "Oh, you'd like that, wouldn't you? So, you can continue your little affair without witnesses?"

"That's enough," a firm voice interjected. It was Ted, who had approached with Maggie. "James, you're not acting rationally. Let's go somewhere quiet."

"Stay out of this!" James snapped, swaying slightly as he glared at Ted.

At that moment, camera flashes went off—a photographer capturing the heated exchange. Then another. The spectacle had drawn the attention of the media present, and cameras began clicking rapidly.

The security team reached James, gently but firmly attempting to escort him away. "Sir, please come with us," one of them said.

He jerked his arm away. "Get your hands off me!"

"James, please," Isabella implored, tears welling up. "You're making it worse."

He looked at her, a mixture of pain and anger etched across his face. "Is this what you wanted? To humiliate me in front of everyone?"

"No, that's not true," she responded softly. "We can talk about this later."

"There's nothing to talk about!" he growled.

The security guards took hold of his arms, and this time he didn't resist, his energy waning. "Let's go, sir," they urged.

As they escorted him away, the murmur of conversations slowly resumed, though the atmosphere remained tense.

Isabella stood frozen, her face pale. Zach placed a comforting hand on her shoulder. "Are you okay?"

She nodded absently, her gaze distant. "I didn't think he'd... not like this."

Maggie stepped forward, wrapping an arm around Isabella. "Come on, let's get some air."

They guided her toward a quieter area, away from prying eyes and the persistent flash of cameras.

***

Meanwhile, in the lower level of the venue, Davina's associate moved with purpose. He approached the secure chamber where the Quantum Bridge was housed, his demeanour calm and unhurried. With a swipe of a keycard—acquired through Davina's machinations—the door unlocked with a soft beep.

Inside, the room was dimly lit, the Quantum Bridge standing at the centre— a low, rhythmic pulse underscoring its dormant power. He moved with precise, practiced ease, his face betraying nothing as he approached the console. The blue glow of the interface bathed his features as he inserted the sleek, unmarked device. The screen flickered briefly, a progress bar slowly filling as data flowed seamlessly into the unknown.

Once the transfer was complete, he disconnected the device, tucking it back into his pocket. Before leaving, he made subtle adjustments to the system settings—minor alterations that would go unnoticed until it was too late.

Exiting the room, he ensured the door locked behind him. His mission accomplished, he blended back into the background, just another face among the many.

He adjusted his cufflinks, the faint metallic click of the console locking behind him the only sound as he exited. With a calm, practiced stride, he rejoined the guests upstairs, another invisible player in Davina's orchestrated game.

Every move had been set; the pieces were in play.

All that remained was to watch the final act unfold.

22 – BRIDGE OF TEARS

"The more we try to control the future, the more fragile the present becomes."

Kongresshaus Zürich Gotthardstrasse 5, 8002 Zürich – 09:15 PM March 29

The maître de cérémonie stepped forward, his smooth baritone voice resonating as he addressed the assembled guests. "Ladies and gentlemen, kindly return to your seats—the keynote speech is about to commence."

A ripple of anticipation filled the hall as guests slowly made their way to their tables, whispers of curiosity filling the air. At the Daystrom table, Ted stood, smoothing his jacket before casting a glance towards Maggie. He gave her a brief, affectionate squeeze, sharing a silent moment.

"Time to shine," she murmured, to which he responded with a warm smile, his eyes gleaming with nervous excitement.

Zach, seated beside Isabella, leaned over, a gentle kiss caressing her cheek, their moment lingering amidst the murmuring crowd.

"Wish me luck," he whispered with a grin, his eyes lit up

with confidence and anticipation.

"You won't need it," Isabella replied, squeezing his hand. "But good luck all the same."

With a final glance at her, he rose and made his way towards the rear of the room, where his team awaited. One of the technicians, visibly nervous, offered a sheepish nod as Zach joined them.

The lights dimmed gradually, casting the room in a soft, ambient glow as a hush fell over the audience. Centre stage now, Ted took his place at the podium, a spotlight illuminating him. He paused momentarily, allowing the silence to settle, before commencing his address.

"Ladies and gentlemen, esteemed guests, honourable members of the scientific community," Ted began his speech, rich and mellow, effortlessly filling the expansive hall. "We gather tonight not merely to celebrate advancements in science but to open a doorway to realms beyond our wildest imaginings. Quantum science holds the key to unlocking unprecedented potential—cures for diseases, leaps in artificial intelligence, the expansion of computational capabilities. These achievements are extraordinary, without doubt, but they merely scratch the surface."

He let his words linger, the tension in the room palpable. "For generations, humanity has dreamed of exploring the stars, yet the distances—the vast chasms of space—

seemed insurmountable, too immense to traverse."

The ripples of hushed voices spilled across the hall, the excitement building with each syllable.

Ted's eyes sparkled as he leaned slightly into the microphone. "Until now."

The room fell utterly silent, all eyes upon him, their collective breath held in anticipation. "Tonight, you will witness the culmination of years of relentless research, countless sleepless nights, and unwavering dedication. We stand on the threshold of a new journey—one that transcends space, time, and the very dimensions we inhabit."

He paused, tracing his eyes over the captivated faces before him. "It is my profound honour to introduce the dawn of a new era. Ladies and gentlemen, I present to you—the Quantum Bridge."

The lighting changed dramatically as ethereal music played softly in the background. The floor beneath the stage began to hum, and with a slow, almost reverent ascent, the Quantum Bridge emerged from its concealed platform. A sleek, futuristic apparatus, its surfaces gleaming under the lights, appeared to levitate above the stage. Zach, now clad in his lab coat, stood beside it, accompanied by the nervous technician who endeavoured to remain unobtrusive.

A collective gasp spread through the audience, their attention wholly captivated by the spectacle before them. The atmosphere tingled with the exhilarating promise of a revolutionary breakthrough.

Ted's voice resonated once more. "What you see before you is not merely the fruit of our labour at Daystrom Biotech. It represents a monumental leap forward in human discovery. This evening, we will make history. We will open a portal—a tiny window—to another universe."

A wave of disbelief and awe swept through the crowd as the magnitude of his statement sank in. This was more than a technological demonstration; it was the unveiling of a discovery that could alter the course of humanity.

The audience sat enthralled, eyes fixed upon the stage, as Ted gestured towards Zach. Approaching the Quantum Bridge, Zach's hands moved with assured precision as he initiated the final preparations. The tension in the air building, every heartbeat synchronised in anticipation of what was to come.

Zach glanced briefly towards the audience, his eyes meeting Isabella's for the briefest of moments. She offered a subtle nod, her heart pounding. He turned back to the device, his fingers deftly manipulating the controls. The machine began to emit a gentle hum, the sound escalating into a steady, rhythmic pulse.

Ted returned to his seat beside Maggie, his face flushed with pride. She smiled reassuringly, sensing the importance of the moment. Across the way, Davina reclined gracefully, her manicured fingers lightly tapping the stem of her champagne flute. She leaned back, her eyes gleaming in anticipation.

The lights dimmed to near darkness, prompting a collective murmur. Then, the room was bathed in a kaleidoscope of flickering lights—amber, red, and brilliant white—dazzling against the darkened stage. The Quantum Bridge, now fully illuminated, commanded attention as shimmering zones of light materialized, ethereal shadows hinting at what lay beyond. The pulses grew deeper and more intense.

Maggie reached across and gently took Isabella's hand, squeezing it as they shared the weight of the moment. Isabella's gaze remained fixed on the bridge, her body tense as the energy level surged.

Maggie leaned over, discreetly passing Isabella a small piece of paper. Isabella glanced curiously at Maggie, then unfolded the note.

You have to decide, it read.

Before Isabella could react, the container at the heart of the bridge began to dematerialize, shimmering as its form dissolved into a luminous haze, its essence entwined with particles from an alternate universe. Gasps rippled through the audience, witnessing what seemed a kind of magic.

A wave of astonishment swept through the hall. On a large screen behind the stage, a digital counter appeared, glowing brightly in the semi-darkness. It began counting down from ten. At eight, the audience, perhaps instinctively, began to count along. "Seven, six, five..." Their collective voice grew louder with each number. When they reached "one," a tense hush descended once more.

Then, as if summoned by their unified anticipation, the container began to rematerialize. Initially a mere flicker, a mirage shimmering into existence, it gradually solidified, becoming clearer, more tangible.

Another surge of gasps, louder this time. The impossible was unfolding before their very eyes.

The container fully reappeared, every atom restored as though it had never departed. The audience erupted into applause—spontaneous, thunderous, imbued with awe and exhilaration.

Zach, standing centre stage, exhaled a deep sigh of relief, a triumphant smile on his face. He cast a discreet glance towards his colleagues. Maggie, Ted, and Isabella exchanged looks of profound satisfaction, their expressions reflecting the enormity of what they had achieved.

But not all shared in the elation.

Davina, still at her table, watched on with a cool detachment, her expression enigmatic. She glanced at her watch before rising with a grace that belied her true intentions. She proceeded towards the exit, pausing before stepping outside, turning to look back at the stage, her eyes narrowing as she regarded Zach amidst the still-resounding applause. The ghost of a smile tugged at the corner of her lips, devoid of warmth.

One of her associates, waiting for her, draped a long, dark coat over her shoulders. She headed toward the exit, anticipation written all over .

***

On stage, a technician reached to deactivate the system, intending to conclude the demonstration. Instead, the power surged, sending a shockwave across the platform. The air vibrated with an intense thud as the light around the bridge flared violently, flickering erratically in darker hues of light. Dread washed over Zach—the bridge was out of control.

"Shut it down!" he yelled, rushing to the console. His hands flew over the controls, desperately attempting to override the system. But the bridge was unresponsive, surging in a feedback loop. The shimmering light around it grew increasingly chaotic. The once-stable boundaries now twisted and warped, dancing unpredictably.

Guests who had moments before been enraptured now sat frozen, watching in disbelief as the Quantum Bridge began to overload. Reality splintering before their eyes, rippling outward like shards of broken glass. Space-time fractured, each shard reflecting infinite possibilities—wonders and terrors alike—swirling in and out of view.

Serene vistas of untouched worlds gave way to nightmares of chaos and destruction. The boundaries of existence blurred, and with every pulse of energy, new, impossible realities flickered into sight before collapsing again, the air shuddering with the sheer force of it all. The room seemed to bend and warp, as if the entire universe were teetering on the verge of oblivion.

The bridge's energy rippled outward, the space around it expanding, growing in intensity. Everything on the stage began to levitate, drawn towards the vortex forming at the core of the bridge. Reality itself seemed to be unravelling. Flashes of light erupted sporadically, and the very ground trembled beneath their feet.

Maggie gasped as a torrent of visions overwhelmed her, her mind assailed by images from worlds not her own. Her grip tightened on Isabella's hand, her knuckles white with fear. She could see it now—how everything was destined to repeat, the loop unfurling again, no matter how hard she tried to alter its course.

She knew her time had come. A bittersweet emotion overcame her. She had tried to save them again, tried to rewrite fate, yet here she was, on the brink once more. The end of one cycle, was the beginning of another. She took one last, longing look of love toward Zach, wishing, even in her defeat, that somehow, she could find the strength to break the cycle one day.

Isabella was succumbing too, the particles of quantum energy from the laboratory spill reinforcing the effects of the bridge on her. Visions flooded her mind—memories from realities that shouldn't exist, yet were real for her, in some other place and time. She somehow managed to find the strength to stand. As she did so, Maggie whispered two words before succumbing.

"Remember me." was all she managed, her smile fading alongside her.

Isabella nodded and turned toward Zach. She pushed through the chaotic throng, dodging panicked guests and debris, fighting her way to the stage. "Zach!" she screamed, her voice drowned beneath the cacophony.

Unseen in the chaos, James had made his way back into the hall, dishevelled and desperate. His eyes locked onto Isabella. The sight of her reaching out to Zach ignited his fury. "Isabella!" he roared, forcing his way through the terrified crowd.

The vortex grew, its unassailable pull intensifying. Ted had returned to the device, frantically attempting to disconnect the power couplings, as he battled against time.

Caught on the *event horizon*, one of the Daystrom team was trapped, her body pulled inexorably toward the bridge. She contorted, every atom in her body stretching into a stream of light as she was sucked across the void. She disappeared in a blinding symphony of light, her energy fuelling the vortex. It surged with newfound intensity, its hunger growing.

Isabella and Zach were both perilously close to the event horizon. They held on to each other, struggling against the overwhelming force threatening to tear them apart. Objects around them were hurled into the air, drawn towards the swirling abyss.

James, unsteady but driven by desperation, stumbled towards them, intent on wrenching Isabella away. But in an instant, the vortex ensnared him as well. His footing gave way, and before he could resist, the force dragged him helplessly forward. His terrified face locked eyes with Isabella, pleading without words. He collided with her and Zach, sending the three of them hurtling toward the horizon as reality itself twisted around them.

Isabella, her heart pounding, reached for Zach's hand, but the pull of the vortex was calling her. As James was yanked violently from her side, she watched in horror her arm outstretched toward him, as he was torn across the bridge. His face contorted with fear, disappearing into another reality—a fractured world he wouldn't comprehend. Her heart ached for him, a man she still cared for, now lost to the infinite folly of the universe.

As the vortex's force intensified, Isabella felt the unbearable tug from both sides. Her love for Zach pulled her toward him, while James, disappearing into the void, still held a piece of her heart. Torn between them, the emotional pressure crushed her, and she screamed, her soul breaking for both men, powerless to stop the chaos consuming them.

In those final moments, clarity struck. She had been paralyzed, caught between her past with James and her future with Zach, unable to choose. She had fought for years with James, fallen deeply for Zach, but now, in this moment of reckoning, she was bound to both.

Maggie's final cryptic words now made sense. Isabella had to remember, had to carry this knowledge forward, so that when she faced this choice again, she could make it with conviction. She had to commit to one path and never look back.

She could see Zach amidst the swirling storm of infinite possibilities. The universes shifted and fractured around them, but in that chaos, she mouthed the same words

Maggie had spoken to her.

"Remember me."

With one final, desperate, wrenching pull, the vortex seized her completely, and she too was dragged across the bridge, falling into the abyss of shattered realities.

"No!" Zach gasped, his eyes wide with horror as she started to fade. He reached out desperately, but it was too late. Her fingers slipped beyond his reach, and in a heartbeat, she was gone.

At that exact moment, Ted severed the power coupling. The bridge emitted a deafening crack, the vortex collapsing upon itself with a harrowing scream. Darkness engulfed the room, the chaos abruptly vanished.

A haunting stillness engulfed the hall. Zach stood motionless, staring at the space where she had been, disbelief etched upon his face. The silence was deafening, masking the devastation left in the wake of the Quantum Bridge disaster.

She left behind choices untaken.

23 – A BITTER SYMPHONY

" True discovery lies not in finding new places but in seeing with fresh eyes."

Kongresshaus Zürich Gotthardstrasse 5, 8002 Zürich – 09:35 PM March 29

The Grand Hall felt hollow, as if every sound had been swallowed by an unseen abyss. The buzz of conversation, the clinking of glasses, the jubilant atmosphere— all had vanished, leaving a suffocating silence that hung over those who remained. The residual energy of the Quantum Bridge had collapsed into itself, an oppressive stillness settling like smouldering ash.

Zach stood motionless, centre stage, where Isabella had stood just moments before. It felt like an eternity had passed. Her presence lingered like a ghostly imprint, just beyond reach. She had been torn from him, pulled into the chaos of the vortex before he could save her. The pain of her loss filled his soul with an aching emptiness that threatened to engulf him entirely.

It was as if his world had shattered, leaving only fragments of a reality he no longer wanted. His mind replayed the scene in agonizing detail: the desperation in Isabella's eyes, the way her fingers had slipped from his grasp, the silent scream that never reached his ears. This was a nightmare from which he could not awaken, a torment that clung to him like a shadow.

His hands gripped the cold metal controls of the Quantum Bridge, knuckles white from the strain. He hadn't moved since Isabella vanished, paralysed in an endless cycle of despair. He wanted to scream, to tear the machine apart, to do anything that might bring her back.

Around him, the room had become an unsettling tableau of shock and bewilderment. A few guests, emboldened by the stillness, peered cautiously around the arched doorway, their faces ashen as if witnessing the aftermath of an unthinkable catastrophe. Eyes wide and mouths agape, they whispered in fragmented sentences, desperately attempting to piece together the madness they had just observed.

Ted's heart pounded in his ears as he staggered to his feet, limbs heavy and uncooperative. His vision blurred while he tried to make sense of the chaos, his mind grasping for explanations that eluded him. Frantically, he turned, searching for something—anything—to anchor him to reality.

"Maggie?" he whispered hoarsely, unable to make himself heard. Where was she?

His eyes darted to where she had been moments before,

her vibrant presence had become a beacon in his life. But now, that light was gone. Panic surged within him as he scanned the room, his heart hammering against his ribcage. She couldn't have simply vanished. Not her as well.

A cold sweat broke out across his forehead, dread tightening its grip around him like a vice. The thought of losing her too was unthinkable. Memories flooded his mind: Maggie's laughter echoing in the lab; the way her eyes sparkled when she solved a complex problem; the soft caress of her touch during late-night walks. The possibility that she was gone filled him with an emotion he had never felt before.

Ted stumbled down from the stage, weaving through scattered debris, broken glass, and overturned chairs. His steps were frantic, uneven. Desperation propelled him from table to table, scouring the stunned faces in a futile search for hers.

"Maggie?" he called out louder this time, overcome with fear. Each unanswered plea intensified the sinking feeling in his stomach. He felt as though he were moving through quicksand, every movement slow and heavy, the world around him distorted and surreal.

In the distance, Zach remained a solitary figure—still and silent—hands braced against the controls of the dormant bridge. Ted's heart twisted at the sight: a man broken, silhouetted against the backdrop of devastation. Consumed by his own search, he had momentarily forgotten about Zach. Now, seeing his colleague standing there, utterly lost, his grief compounded.

"Zach!" Ted's voice wavered as he approached the stage once more. His legs felt like lead, the troubles of the world carried on his shoulders. Climbing the steps was an arduous task, each one steeper than the last. The enormity of their loss threatened to crush him.

Zach did not respond. His head was bowed, shoulders slumped, eyes fixed on the floor. A chill coursed through Ted; he had never seen Zach so defeated, so utterly heartbroken.

"Zach..." he repeated softly, placing a trembling hand on his friend's shoulder. The gesture was meant to comfort, but Zach remained unresponsive. His eyes, red-rimmed and vacant, stared unseeingly at the controls, as if willing the bridge to offer answers or a means to reverse the horrors that had transpired.

"I couldn't save her," Zach cried out, his whole being raw with anguish. "She was right there, Ted. Right there, and I couldn't... I couldn't hold on to her." His hands shook violently, the memory of Isabella's touch an agonizing phantom sensation.

Ted swallowed hard, his throat tight with emotion. Words failed him. What solace could he offer when he himself was drowning in despair? They had all witnessed the same nightmare unfold. A deep sense of helplessness washed over him, and he wished desperately that he could turn back time, undo the chain of events that had led them to this abyss.

"We'll... we'll figure this out, Zach," he managed to say, though his words felt hollow and insufficient. "We can't give up." But even as he spoke, doubt ate at the edges of his resolve. How could they fix this? How could they bring them back from the unknown reaches of wherever they had vanished?

Zach shook his head slowly, a gesture heavy with despair. "She's gone," he uttered, the finality in his tone chilling. "Isabella's gone. I let her slip away."

A tear traced a solitary path down Zach's cheek, but he made no move to wipe it away. The guilt of what had happened crushing him. He had promised himself he would protect her, that he would never let harm come to her. And now, she was lost because of him.

Ted's own heart felt ripped apart, Zach's grief was unbearable. He scanned the room, the faces of the few who had dared to return were pallid, their eyes filled with disbelief. Those who remained had hands pressed to their mouths, their whispers a muted chorus of fear and confusion. Fragments of conversations reached his ears, each one only deepening the surreal sense of unreality.

"It's over," Zach said, the emptiness he felt echoing in the silent hall. "Everything we worked for... everything we dreamed of... it's all over."

Ted opened his mouth to respond, but no words came. Despair seeped into his very bones. His mind, overwhelmed by thoughts of Maggie's disappearance and Isabella's loss, struggled to hold onto any semblance of hope. The project that had once filled them with inspiration and excitement had become a source of unimaginable pain.

Zach closed his eyes, fighting back a tide of emotion that threatened to consume him entirely. He had failed her—failed to protect the woman he loved. And now she was gone, beyond reach, swallowed by a reality he could not comprehend.

Yet amidst the collapse of the Quantum Bridge, something lingered—a trace, a faint ripple in the air, as though the fracture had left a scar upon the very fabric of existence. The instability had not fully dissipated. Even with both Isabella and Maggie lost, the ordeal was far from concluded.

"Zach," Ted said quietly, striving to inject a note of resolve into the proceedings. "We need to find them. We need to understand what happened. This isn't the end. It can't be the end."

Zach's eyes opened slowly, determination piercing through the haze of grief. The thought of Isabella lost somewhere—perhaps frightened, perhaps alone—stirred something deep within him. He could not abandon her. He would not.

"We have to get them back," he murmured, his tone tinged with newfound resolve. "You're right. I can't... I won't let this be the end."

Ted grasped his friend's shoulder more firmly, though uncertainty gnawed at his own heart. He had no idea where to begin, but he knew they couldn't surrender to despair. They couldn't leave those women—brilliant minds, irreplaceable souls—lost in the void.

"We'll figure it out," Ted said more firmly. "Together. We'll find a way."

Zach met his gaze, the spark of hope igniting in his eyes. "We need to analyse the data," he said, his scientific mind reasserting itself. "There must be something—some anomaly, some trace—that can help us understand where they went."

Ted nodded. "The equipment should have recorded the fluctuations. If we can understand what caused the bridge to destabilise, perhaps we can reverse it, bring them back."

An air of resolve began to replace the numbness. Action was better than despair. They had to try.

***

Obsidian Biotech, The Tower, 1 St. George Wharf, Vauxhall, London SW8 2DA – Previously, 09:34 PM, January 29

James hit the ground with a jarring thud, the impact driving the breath from his lungs. Pain exploded across his back as he lay sprawled on an unyielding surface. Dazed, he struggled to orient himself. The world spun around him in a dizzying blur, and for a terrifying moment, he feared he might lose consciousness. His head throbbed mercilessly as he blinked against the harsh, sterile light overhead. Where was he?

Attempting to stand, he was abruptly hauled to his feet by hands that gripped his arms with iron strength. Gasping, his senses awash with confusion and mounting panic, James took in his surroundings. The men flanking him were imposing figures—towering, stone-faced, their expressions impassive as they held him firmly in place. Their silence was menacing, a wordless warning that escape was futile.

As they steadied him, he caught sight of her.

Davina Drake.

She sat at her desk, a short distance away, exuding an aura of cold authority. Arms folded elegantly, a sly smile played on her ruby lips. Her eyes roamed over him with a familiar, predatory look, satisfaction gleaming in their depths. The sleek lines of her attire mirrored the stark yet luxurious environment—a realm where she reigned supreme.

"James," she drawled, her voice slicing through the haze like a blade of ice. "So glad you could join us. Took your time, didn't you?"

He stared at her, bewilderment mingling with a deepening apprehension. What was she doing here? His heart raced, each beat echoing like a drum in his ears. Forcing himself to speak, all he could think of was, "Where... where am I?"

Davina tilted her head ever so slightly, her amusement clear to see. "Let's just say things operate a bit differently *here*." She began to circle him with measured, deliberate steps, like a predator assessing its prey. "You took your sweet time arriving, but don't fret. I knew you'd show up eventually. You always do."

Swallowing hard, the unease coiled within him. Davina exuded a ruthless cunning that set his nerves on edge. The room around him was unfamiliar—sterile walls gleamed under harsh lighting, and the air carried an undercurrent of menace. "What happened to me?" he managed to utter, his throat dry.

Her smile widened, devoid of warmth. "My darling James, you did exactly what was asked of you. You did what I wanted." She paused, her gaze piercing into his. "And now you're here, with me. Don't you recognise me?" She let out a cold, mirthless laugh. "You really don't know, do you?" Her words promised nothing good to come.

"Welcome to my reality. Your new home—for the time being," she added with a dismissive wave of her hand. She stared at him intently, her steely gaze piercing his very soul. The scale of her revelation was a hammer blow.

"Oh, no..." was all he could muster, the dawning realization of his situation sinking in like a stone. A chill raced down his spine as comprehension flooded his mind.

Did you seriously think I'd fail to control something as potent as the Quantum Bridge? In this reality, I've achieved precisely what I set out to do a long time ago. The bridge is mine here, and soon it will be mine everywhere."

A cold dread embraced him, squeezing the air from his lungs. He saw her unyielding ambition—the insatiable hunger for power without restraint or morality. Memories of his own failures flooded back; the jealousy that had consumed him, the reckless actions that had led him down a path of destruction. Guilt and regret twisted like knives within him.

"What do you want from me?" he asked, a tremor betraying the fear he desperately tried to suppress. His mind raced, but beneath the terror lay a seed of defiance. He had been manipulated before; he would not be a pawn again.

Her laughter was sharp, echoing with disdain. "Want from you?" She circled him slowly, her eyes never leaving his face. "You've proven yourself to be... malleable, James. A pawn in every reality. But even pawns have their uses." She stopped directly in front of him, her smile turning icy. "You're eager to return to your dear Isabella, aren't you?"

His breath hitched at the mention of her name. The image of Isabella's face flashed before him—her eyes filled with sorrow. He realised with crushing clarity how deeply he had hurt her, how his own insecurities had driven a wedge between them. "I need to go back. I have to make things right," he pleaded, desperation seeping into his words like poison.

Davina's eyes glittered with triumph. "I'm sure you do." She leaned in closer, her voice dropping to a whisper. "But here's the catch—you won't be going anywhere unless you do something for me."

"And what's that?" His question was tinged in dread. He felt trapped, the hopelessness of it all washing over him. Was he destined to make the same mistakes over and over, ensnared in a cycle he could not break?

She brushed a finger along his cheek, her graze mocking and possessive. "I desire control, James. Not just here, but across all realities. And you... you're going to help me achieve that."

He recoiled, dread coiling in his stomach like a serpent. "I won't help you hurt her," he said fiercely, mustering what courage he could. "I won't be part of your schemes."

Davina's smirk deepened, her eyes narrowing. "Oh, but you will. You see, you don't really have a choice." She stepped back, her gaze locking onto his with a predatory intensity. "You're making the same mistakes that led you here—desperate, willing to bargain away your soul for something you've already lost."

Shame and frustration warred within him. He knew she was manipulating him, yet felt powerless to resist. The thought of being trapped here, never seeing Isabella again, was unbearable. "What choice do I have?" he whispered, defeat now his ghostly companion.

"Precisely," she purred, satisfaction dripping from every syllable. "Now, be a good pawn and do as you're told." She retrieved a small device from her pocket—a sleek, ominous object that pulsed with a faint, eerie light. The same he'd seen on the stage before..."

Recognition flashed in his eyes. "The Bridge..." he murmured, his heart lurching.

"Indeed." She regarded the device with a possessive air, her fingers caressing its surface. "You're going back to your world, James. Back to your beloved wife. But this time, I'll be the one pulling the strings from the start." Her gaze bored into him, malice gleaming like cold steel.

Despair settled over him like a heavy cloak, suffocating and inescapable. He wanted to rebel, to fight, but his limbs felt leaden, drained of strength. "Why are you doing this?" he asked, anger piercing through his fear. "What do you gain from causing so much pain?"

Her expression hardened, eyes narrowing to slits. "Power, James. Control. And the satisfaction of seeing those who underestimated me brought to their knees." She paused, the sound of her voice almost venomous. "It's just a matter of time."

Before he could respond, she pressed a button on the device. The ground beneath him seemed to lurch violently, the very fabric of reality shifting and contorting. His vision blurred as an invisible force yanked him backward, a vertiginous sensation of falling enveloping him like a dark embrace.

Panic surged through his veins. "Davina!" he shouted, reaching out instinctively, but his fingers grasped only empty air.

Her face was the last thing he saw—a cold, triumphant smile etched upon it. "Off you go again. See you on the other side." she murmured, her voice echoing hauntingly as the world around him dissolved into darkness.

James plunged into the abyss, terror gripping him with icy fingers as the Quantum Bridge swallowed him whole. The void enveloped him, a swirling maelstrom of thoughts and emotions spiralling chaotically. Regret consumed him—regret for his actions, for allowing jealousy to cloud his judgment, for becoming a pawn once more in an endless game he scarcely understood.

As he tumbled through the darkness, a single thought anchored him amidst the chaos: he had to find a way home. Not just to his world, but to redemption. To prove that he was more than a pawn, more than the sum of his mistakes.

Once more into the fray, dear James.

24 – A PATH WELL-TRODDEN

"Not until we are lost do we begin to understand ourselves."

Somewhere else. Another time, another place

The world around Isabella was a tangled web of contradictions—both foreign and intimately familiar. She stood in the middle of an empty street, the asphalt cool beneath her feet. Buildings loomed on either side, their façades shimmering as if seen through a veil of water. It was as if she had stepped into a painting where the artist couldn't decide between reality and abstraction.

There was only silence. The stillness was unsettling, as if time itself had paused to observe her bewilderment. Isabella's breath came in shallow bursts. Her eyes darted from one distorted landmark to another, each a twisted echo of places she knew. Everything felt suspended, hovering between existence and illusion.

The magnitude of her recent decisions crushed like a press. She had made the ultimate sacrifice, throwing herself into the heart of chaos to prevent it from consuming everything she held dear. Yet now, standing in this fractured version of reality, doubt consumed her. Had she succeeded, or merely exchanged one form of turmoil for another? The streets, the buildings, even the sky—they all seemed familiar yet fundamentally wrong, as though she were viewing the world through a cracked mirror.

A soft breeze swept through the deserted avenue, carrying with it the faintest whispers of voices. They drifted around her like remnants of forgotten songs, notes of melancholy and hope interwoven. Her heart pounded as she turned, catching fleeting glimpses of figures at the periphery of her vision. The voices were distorted but achingly familiar, like echoes from a long-forgotten dream.

"Isabella..."

Her name floated on the air, both a comfort and a haunting. It was soft yet unsettling, imbued with layers of emotion she couldn't immediately unravel. Every instinct urged her to flee, to escape whatever spectral presence was reaching out to her. Yet she remained rooted to the spot, compelled by an inexplicable pull. Slowly, almost against her will, she turned toward the voice.

Standing a few paces away was a woman—older, with eyes that mirrored her own. Lines of wisdom and sorrow etched her face, but serenity emanated from her, defying the dissonance of their surroundings. It was like gazing into a future she hadn't yet lived but somehow remembered.

"Who are you?" Isabella asked, incredulous.

The older woman's gaze held hers steadily. "You've been here before," she said softly, her voice carrying the cost of countless unspoken truths. It was as though she had been waiting for this moment, for this convergence of their paths.

Isabella's mind reeled. A thousand questions surged forward, colliding and tangling until none could escape her lips. Fear mingled with curiosity, creating a tumultuous storm within her. "What is this? Where am I?" she finally managed to ask, her voice trembling.

The woman's smile was tinged with a sadness that resonated deep within her. "You're where you've always been—caught between the choices you've made and those you still haven't. These aren't just fractures in time; they're reflections of you. Reflections of possible tomorrows."

Panic rose within her, threatening to spill over. Isabella turned her head in a desperate attempt to escape the disquieting truth. "I don't understand," she stammered, voice trembling. "I made my choice. I was certain I had..."

The woman took a gentle step closer, her presence both comforting and unsettling. She showed a depth of feeling—a well of understanding that seemed to encompass all of Isabella's fears and doubts.

"Are you sure? Did you really choose? Try to remember," she said. "The memories you've seen—they're more than mere shadows. They're pathways, alternate realities that exist alongside your own. They are the choices you've yet to make, or those you decided against."

Head spinning. she squeezed her eyes shut, trying to steady herself. The enormity of the woman's words pressed down upon her. Her dreams—the vivid visions of lives unlived, of moments with Zach that felt as real as her own heartbeat—they weren't just figments of her imagination. They were echoes of possibilities, threads of alternate existences woven alongside her own.

Every road not taken, every decision unmade, had left behind fragments—pieces of herself scattered across the vast tapestry of reality. "I'm trapped," she uttered, the admission tearing her apart. "Destined to repeat the same life, over and over again."

The woman's expression softened, her own pain reflected in the crease of her brow. "No, Isabella," she replied gently. "You're not trapped. You're awakening to the fullness of who you are. In time, you will remember. You will learn."

A tremor ran through Isabella's body. "But I don't want this," she cried, a tear slipping down her cheek. "I can't live like this. Infinite possibilities. Living through every version of myself."

"None of us can," the woman agreed. "But acknowledging their existence doesn't mean you have to live them all. It means embracing the complexity of your soul—the myriad of paths that shape who you are, and finally choosing which path to take, once and for all."

Isabella's thoughts churned. The life she wanted with Zach had felt so close, within touching distance. She had hesitated, torn between certainty and the unknown. And so, here she was, confronted with the reality that those echoes were an intrinsic part of her being.

"What are you showing me?" she asked, her voice raw with emotion. "Why can't I just live my life without these shadows haunting me?"

The woman reached out, her hand hovering before settling gently on Isabella's shoulder. Her touch was warm, affectionate. "Because to deny them is to deny a part of yourself," she said softly. "The choices we make don't erase the ones we didn't. They coexist, shaping us in ways we might not immediately understand. These remnants—they are part of your story."

Isabella looked into the woman's eyes and saw her own reflection—a mosaic of joy and sorrow, triumph and regret. The barriers she had erected around her heart began to crumble. "I thought I was free," she murmured, her defences faltering. "I thought choosing meant leaving all this behind."

"Freedom isn't about running from what was or what could have been," the woman replied. "It's about embracing all that you are—the known and the unknown, the seen and unseen. Only then can you truly move forward."

Silence descended upon them. Isabella felt a shift within—a loosening of the knots that had bound her. The fear that had gripped her began to ebb, replaced by a tentative acceptance.

"I don't know how to live with this knowledge," she admitted. "How do I move forward, knowing there are parts of me scattered across realities I can't touch?"

The woman's smile was gentle, her eyes shining with unshed tears. "By trusting yourself," she said simply. "By understanding that while those paths exist, they don't diminish the one you're on. They enrich it. You carry their lessons, their wisdom, even if you don't walk their roads."

Isabella let the air to fill her lungs and calmed herself. She considered the lives she had glimpsed—the love, the pain, the countless moments that weren't hers yet felt intimately familiar. Gone were the fears the once held. Now they were simply stories, chapters in a grander narrative.

"Perhaps I've been afraid of taking that last step," she said quietly. "Afraid to acknowledge that my choices are what truly matter to me."

The woman nodded. "We all fear what we don't fully understand. But it's in embracing our complexities that we find true peace."

A newfound clarity began to dawn within Isabella. The turmoil that had once consumed her felt like a turbulent sea finally calming. She realised that she didn't have to fight the echoes or flee from them. She could let them be, allow them to exist without letting them dictate her choices.

"Thank you," she said. Gratitude welled up inside her—not just for the woman before her, but for the parts of herself she was finally accepting.

The woman stepped back, her form beginning to shimmer at the edges. "This is your journey now, Isabella. Trust in it. Trust in yourself."

Before Isabella could say another word, the woman faded, dissolving into the ambient light until she was just another memory. Perhaps that was all she had ever been.

Isabella stood alone on the empty street, the silence now imbued with a future filled with possibilities rather than dread. The air around her felt lighter, the distorted buildings less ominous.

Her gaze softened, and she let her eyes close, allowing a quiet peace to settle over her. The other versions of herself—the alternate lives and the moments left unlived—were there, woven into her being, a part of her now.

When she opened her eyes, the world around her began to shift. Colours brightened, edges sharpened, and the unsettling haze lifted. The street transformed into one she recognised unmistakably—the street where she and Zach had shared countless walks, where laughter and conversation flowed freely.

A soft warmth spread through her. She knew what she had to do.

***

The residence of Isabella and Zach Mondori, Russell Square Mansions, 12 Russell Square, Bloomsbury, London, WC1B 5BG, another time.

Morning light filtered softly through the windows, casting hues of gold throughout the room. Isabella opened her eyes to the familiar surroundings of her bedroom. The gentle sounds of the city awakening drifted in—the distant hum of traffic, the chirping of birds, the rustling of leaves in the breeze.

She lay still, the remnants of her dream—or whatever it had been—lingering at the edges of her mind. A profound calm had settled within—a tranquillity that had eluded her for so long. Echoes of past disruptions remained, woven seamlessly into the mosaic of her story, integral to who she had become.

She had spent much of her life running—from the past, from disorienting moments, from herself. But now, as the sun ascended over the horizon, painting the sky in hues of rose and amber, Isabella realised she no longer needed to flee. She had faced uncertainties, navigated the labyrinth of endless possibilities, and emerged stronger, more certain of her identity and the path ahead.

Her former choices no longer defined her; she was the author of her own narrative.

A gentle knock at the door interrupted her reverie. She sat up as Zach peeked in, a tender smile gracing his features. A warmth resided in his eyes—a depth that had always been there but now felt profound, enriched by all they had endured together.

"Good morning," he greeted softly. "Hope I didn't wake you."

She shook her head, returning his smile. "No, I was just thinking."

He crossed the room, settling beside her. "Good thoughts, I hope."

"Yes," she replied, her voice filled with serene confidence. "Very good thoughts."

He took her hand, intertwining his fingers with hers. "You seem different—lighter."

She nodded slowly. "I feel... liberated. Like I've finally made peace with myself."

His eyes searched hers, understanding dawning. "That's wonderful, Isabella."

They sat in companionable silence, their shared history hanging lightly between them. There had been times when their world seemed about to collapse, when the burden of their choices felt insurmountable. But now, Isabella understood they had emerged stronger—not just as individuals, but together.

She had chosen him, but more importantly, she had chosen herself. She had embraced life's uncertainties, accepted the remnants of her past as threads in her story, yet no longer allowed them to dictate her journey.

A subtle vibration interrupted the quietude—the phone on the bedside table buzzed, its screen illuminating with a message from Ted:

Data looks promising. Stability achieved. Let's meet later to discuss.

Zach glanced at the message, and with a light-hearted smile said, "Seems Ted is already immersed in work."

Isabella chuckled softly. "He always is."

Once, the fractures of their experiences had consumed Ted, occupying his every thought. But now, even he seemed lighter, unburdened. He had rediscovered his purpose, adapting to the new reality.

She set the phone aside, turning back to Zach. "We should get ready."

He nodded. "A new day awaits."

She stood, stretching, feeling the warmth of the sun on her skin. As she dressed, a quiet contentedness stirred within her—that which had been absent for too long had finally returned.

"Ready to face whatever comes?" Zach asked, pulling on his jacket.

She caught his gaze, her eyes an expression of the calm that had settled within her. "Yes. Together."

He smiled, offering his hand. "Together, forever."

They left the apartment, stepping into the vibrant energy of the city. The world outside awaited, brimming with life's uncertainties and potentials.

As they walked down the street, familiar sounds and sights enveloped them. Isabella felt a profound peace. The future stretched out before her—not as a single, unchangeable path, but as a landscape of possibilities she was free to explore. And she would face it all with an open heart, grounded in the knowledge of who she was.

She had found her way back—not just to her world, but to herself.

***

The Dolce Vita Café, 2A Kensington High Street, London W8 4PT, another time.

Isabella and Zach continued down the bustling avenue, the morning sun embracing another beautiful day. The smell of freshly brewed coffee drifted from the nearby café—their favourite retreat. Without a word, they turned toward it, the bell above the door chiming softly as they entered.

Inside, the familiar hum of conversations and the clatter of cups created a comforting backdrop. They settled into their usual table by the window, the one where they had shared countless moments of laughter and deep conversation.

"Feels like ages since we've been here," Zach remarked, glancing around.

She smiled softly. "It does. But it also feels like coming home."

He reached across, his fingers brushing hers. "I'm glad we're here together."

"Me too," she replied, her sincerity shining through.

As they sipped their coffees, Isabella gazed out at the world beyond the glass—a world alive with endless possibilities.

"Do you ever wonder about the paths we didn't take?" she asked.

Zach considered her question thoughtfully. "Sometimes. But I believe every choice led us to this moment. And I wouldn't trade it for anything."

She nodded, a contented smile spreading across her face. "Neither would I."

He looked at her with gentle curiosity. "What brought this on?"

She took a deep breath, choosing her words carefully. "I think I've been holding onto too many 'what ifs.' But I've realised that embracing who I am now—the choices I've made, the life we're building—that's what truly matters."

He squeezed her hand reassuringly. "I'm happy you've found that peace."

"Thank you," she whispered. "for being patient with me."

"Always," he replied softly.

Their conversation shifted to lighter topics—the day's plans, friends they hadn't seen in a while, places they'd like to visit. The doubt that had once followed them had gone, replaced by a shared optimism.

As they left, Isabella glanced back at the café, committing the scene to memory. It was more than just a place; it was a symbol of new beginnings.

Stepping back onto the street, they walked arm in arm toward the Daystrom Institute. The path ahead was unknown, but they faced it with confidence and unity.

"Do you think Ted will be surprised by our ideas?" Zach asked with a playful grin.

She laughed lightly. "Probably. But he'll come around. He always does."

"True," Zach agreed. "And with the stability data looking good, who knows what breakthroughs await?"

Isabella looked up at the clear blue sky. "I'm ready for whatever comes next."

He kissed her forehead gently. "So am I."

They continued onward, the city alive around them. Each step carried them further into a future they were eager to embrace.

Isabella knew there would be challenges—there always were. But now, she felt equipped to handle them, grounded in self-awareness and strengthened by the bonds she cherished.

As they approached the Institute, the grand twin towers standing as a testament to human ingenuity, Isabella could feel the anticipation building. The echoes of the past had found their place, and the future was hers to live fully.

Embrace not the fear of the unknown, but the promise of infinite possibilities.

EPILOGUE

"In making our choices, we find the paths that lead us to where we're meant to be."

The residence of Isabella Margaret Mondori (née Carter), Russell Square Mansions, 12 Russell Square, Bloomsbury, London, WC1B 5BG – Later in life.

The apartment was quiet, bathed in the soft glow of the setting sun. Isabella stood before the ornate mirror in her bedroom, gazing at her reflection. Time had etched its passage upon her face—silver strands woven through her hair, fine lines tracing stories at the corners of her eyes. Yet her eyes held a depth, a testament to a life fully lived. The echoes of Zach, of James, of other timelines, had softened over the years, settling like distant memories. Still, they lingered, as faint and elusive as shadows at twilight.

She tugged at her hair and sighed softly. The world had found its balance again. The instability that once threatened to unravel everything had settled; life had returned to normalcy. Research continued, but the disturbances had ceased since the collapse of the Bridge. It seemed that time had healed its own wounds.

Yet, as she stared at her reflection, an unsettling

sensation stirred—a feeling that something lay just beyond her perception.

Her eyes traced the familiar contours of her face. The mirror had always been a silent confidant, reflecting her transformations. But now, there was something different. Leaning closer, she noticed a subtle flicker at the mirror's edge.

She froze, heart quickening. For an instant, she thought she saw movement behind her. Spinning around, she found the room empty, just as it had always been. The quiet pressed in around her, yet the sense of being observed remained.

Turning back to the mirror, her reflection met her gaze steadily. But as she peered deeper, a faint ripple disturbed the glass, as though the very air trembled.

An unbidden memory surfaced—the unstable periods, glimpses of alternate lives, versions of herself existing in other realities. For years, she had believed herself free from those episodes, that the divergent paths had closed when equilibrium was restored. But now, standing here, doubt crept in.

Her hand hovered above the cool surface. "Am I truly free?" she whispered into the silence.

The mirror offered no reply, reflecting only her contemplative face. Yet there was something indefinable in her reflection—hiding in the shadows, an unease she couldn't name.

Stepping back, a nervous energy surged through her. She had moved past the turmoil, she reminded herself. She had lived her life, made her choices, left that chaos behind. But the feeling persisted—that the past disruptions had not entirely released their hold.

The apartment felt stifling in its quiet. Seeking solace, Isabella crossed to the window, gazing out over the city. The urban landscape stretched before her, alive with the hum of traffic and distant murmurs. It was an ordinary evening; everything appeared as it should.

Yet the doubt still lingered. What if those temporal rifts hadn't been sealed completely? What if, in some other reality, she was the same woman in a different life, ensnared in an endless web of choices?

Closing her eyes, she pressed her forehead against the cool glass. The disturbances were gone, she reassured herself. Gone.

And yet...

Opening her eyes, she glimpsed movement in the window's reflection. It was faint, almost imperceptible—a figure standing just behind her. Her heart raced as she turned sharply, eyes scanning the room.

Nothing. Only silence greeted her.

Slowly, she turned back to the mirror, her gaze wary. The room was unchanged, but as she faced her reflection, she saw it—a fleeting, haunting figure. A woman—herself, perhaps? Or was it? Taller, slightly different, with an unsettling smile and sharp eyes. A faint ripple distorted the edges, like time itself was fraying. The figure shifted, holding something in her hand. And then, she vanished.

She inhaled sharply, hand trembling. Was this real, or a trick of the mind—a lingering echo of past instabilities? Uncertainty gripped her. The disruptions were supposed to be contained.

A faint breeze stirred the curtains, drawing her attention back to the window. The city lay unchanged, steadfast. But the sense of something unseen, hovering just beyond reach, remained.

She stood there for a long while, eyes locked with her reflection, half-expecting the echoes of other lives to reach out once more. But nothing stirred. The mirror remained still, unyielding.

As the sun dipped below the horizon, Isabella Margaret Carter turned away. She had travelled so far, fought so hard to reclaim her life. And yet, endless possibilities and different paths still clung to the fringes of her existence. How many choices remained for her to make?

Standing by the window as twilight enveloped the city, a passing thought caressed her.

Tomorrow would bring a new day, a *New Dawn*.

AUTHOR'S NOTE

In the quiet hours when the city sleeps and shadows dance upon the walls, I find myself enveloped by the whispers of those who have walked beside me on this winding path. To those who know me not just by name but by the silent language of shared dreams and unspoken truths, I offer my deepest gratitude. Your faith has been the lantern that guides me through the labyrinth of my own making.

To the souls who have woven their threads into the patchwork of my existence—friends who are family, and family who are friends—your patience has been the gentle tide that carries me towards distant horizons. You have stood at the crossroads, waiting with a smile or a knowing glance, as I chased the echoes of stories yet to be told. Your belief in me has been the compass by which I navigate the tumultuous seas of aspiration.

For those who have touched my life from afar, like stars whose light reaches across the vastness to illuminate the night, your influence is etched into the very fabric of my being. Distance may veil our connections, but the resonance of your presence is felt in every step I take towards the dawn.

And to the wanderers, the seekers of truth and beauty

who traverse the hidden corridors of the world, thank you for reminding me that the journey is as vital as the destination. It is in the pursuit of the unknown, in the embrace of mystery and wonder, that we discover the deepest parts of ourselves.

May the winds of fate carry my humble words to you all, a tribute to the roles you have played in this odyssey of the heart and mind. Without you, these pages would be but silent ink upon a barren canvas. With you, they become a symphony—a testament to the enduring power of love, hope, and the relentless pursuit of dreams.

Mark Stone